"What o[...]
about tha[...] so happy?

"You," Stephen said. He was standing beside her, and Suzanne felt the warmth of his forearm against her wrist. She noticed the way his smile lit up his whole face. Like baby Alice's smile. Slowly she was beginning to lose that instinctive mistrust she'd had on first meeting him. Maybe here, at last, was someone else who cared about her orphaned niece.

"She's dreaming about your voice," he continued. "Your fragrance. The songs you sing to her."

They were both watching the baby again, intent on every tiny movement in her face.

"Am I right thinking you would give almost anything to be able to bring her up as your own?" Stephen asked suddenly.

"Of course I would," Suzanne answered. "I love her."

"Then marry me."

Dear Reader,

What are your New Year's resolutions? I hope one is to relax and escape life's everyday stresses with our fantasy-filled books! Each month, Silhouette Romance presents six soul-stirring stories about falling in love. So even if you haven't gotten around to your other resolutions (hey, spring cleaning is still months away!), curling up with these dreamy stories should be one that's a pure pleasure to keep.

Could you imagine seducing the boss? Well, that's what the heroine of Julianna Morris's *Last Chance for Baby*, the fourth in the madly popular miniseries HAVING THE BOSS'S BABY did. And that's what starts the fun in Susan Meier's *The Boss's Urgent Proposal*—part of our AN OLDER MAN thematic series—when the boss... finally...shows up on his secretary's doorstep.

Looking for a modern-day fairy tale? Then you'll adore Lilian Darcy's *Finding Her Prince*, the third in her CINDERELLA CONSPIRACY series about three sisters finding true love by the stroke of midnight! And delight in DeAnna Talcott's I-need-a-miracle tale, *The Nanny & Her Scrooge*.

With over one hundred books in print, Marie Ferrarella is still whipping up fun, steamy romances, this time with three adorable bambinos on board in *A Triple Threat to Bachelorhood*. Meanwhile, a single mom's secret baby could lead to Texas-size trouble in Linda Goodnight's *For Her Child...*, a fireworks-filled cowboy romance!

So, a thought just occurred: Is it cheating if one of your New Year's resolutions is pure fun? Hmm...I don't think so. So kick back, relax and enjoy. You deserve it!

Happy reading!

Mary-Theresa Hussey

Mary-Theresa Hussey
Senior Editor

Please address questions and book requests to:
Silhouette Reader Service
U.S.: 3010 Walden Ave., P.O. Box 1325, Buffalo, NY 14269
Canadian: P.O. Box 609, Fort Erie, Ont. L2A 5X3

Finding Her Prince

LILIAN DARCY

SILHOUETTE *Romance*®
Published by Silhouette Books
America's Publisher of Contemporary Romance

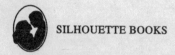

SILHOUETTE BOOKS

ISBN 0-373-19567-2

FINDING HER PRINCE

Visit Silhouette at www.eHarlequin.com

Printed in U.S.A.

LILIAN DARCY

has written nearly fifty books for Silhouette Romance and Harlequin Mills & Boon Medical Romance (Prescription Romance). Her first book for Silhouette appeared on the Waldenbooks Series Romance Bestsellers list, and she's hoping readers go on responding strongly to her work. Happily married, with four active children and a very patient cat, she enjoys keeping busy and could probably fill several more lifetimes with the things she likes to do—including cooking, gardening, quilting, drawing and traveling. She currently lives in Australia but travels to the United States as often as possible to visit family. She loves to hear from fans, who can e-mail her at darcy@dynamite.com.au.

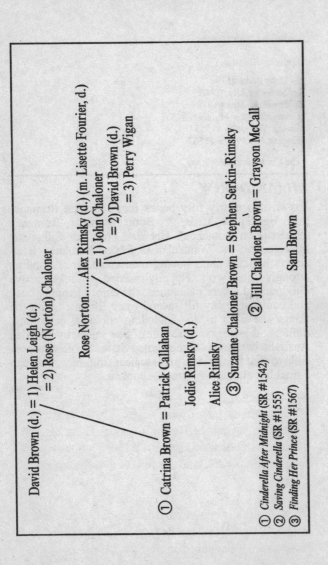

David Brown (d.) = 1) Helen Leigh (d.)
　　　　　　　 = 2) Rose (Norton) Chaloner

Rose Norton.....Alex Rimsky (d.) (m. Lisette Fourier, d.)
　　　　　　　 = 1) John Chaloner
　　　　　　　 = 2) David Brown (d.)
　　　　　　　 = 3) Perry Wigan

① Catrina Brown = Patrick Callahan

Jodie Rimsky (d.)

Alice Rimsky

③ Suzanne Chaloner Brown = Stephen Serkin-Rimsky

② Jill Chaloner Brown = Grayson McCall

Sam Brown

① *Cinderella After Midnight* (SR #1542)
② *Saving Cinderella* (SR #1555)
③ *Finding Her Prince* (SR #1567)

Chapter One

"Darn it, Prince Charming was right!" Suzanne Brown muttered.

She scrunched a small piece of pink, hand-knitted wool in her hand and slashed a line through another of the male names in her appointment diary. This one was Robert. Over the past two days, there had also been Mike, Duane, Les, Colin and Dan. She hadn't spent long enough with any of them to find out their last names.

Her stomach ached and knotted with disappointment. The squeak of Robert's footsteps on the polished vinyl floor faded into the ambient sounds of the busy hospital café, and he left without a backward glance.

Again!

It was the tiny pink baby bootie, still scrunched in her hand, that nixed the deal every single time! And every time, it happened in exactly the same way.

First, Suzanne would rummage in her purse in search of a tissue. Then she would "accidentally" let the bootie fall out of her messy purse onto the coffee shop table. Every time, it looked so cute and fragile, and every time it earned a slightly alarmed stare from the man—Mike, Les, Colin and the others—across the table.

"Are you a single mom, or something?" a couple of them had said.

Picking the bootie up—nervous, at this point—Suzanne would use it as a way to explain the situation with baby Alice.

That her birth mother, Suzanne's much older half sister, Dr. Jodie Rimsky, had died of a brain aneurysm in the sixth month of her pregnancy. That Alice had been safely delivered, more than three months premature, by emergency Caesarean, thanks only to the quick thinking of Jodie's medical practice partner, Michael Feldman.

That Alice was still in hospital and Suzanne was hoping for custody, once the baby was discharged. Alice had been conceived through artificial insemination at a clinic and there was no father to claim her.

Finally, after ten minutes or so, with the pink bootie still cradled in her palm, Suzanne would sit back and watch another chance at Alice's happiness dissolve before her eyes as another near-stranger made his excuses and left.

Up until now, she had never felt much of a personal affinity for the Cinderella fairy tale. In contrast, her sister Jill and stepsister Catrina had developed a magical connection to the girl in the glass slippers just lately. Suzanne couldn't imagine she'd ever share their sense of connection with Cinderella herself. Her feet were pretty large, and she had no glittering balls looming on her social calendar, for a start.

But suddenly, yes, she knew *exactly* how Prince Charming had felt, and she totally agreed with the man's thinking on the issue.

The shoe—or in this case, the little pink bootie—was the deal breaker. If the shoe didn't fit, the date was off.

Suzanne's personal ad had appeared in the latest issue of a well-known New York magazine. Carefully worded, it hadn't alluded to her pressing need for marriage. Every man who responded to it, however, had made it very clear, very early on, that little pink booties didn't fit. Not in his heart. Not in his plans. Not anywhere. Not when those pink booties belonged to a tiny, orphaned premature baby, who was still in the hospital's neonatal intensive care unit.

Suzanne dropped the bootie back onto the coffee shop table in front of her and stared at it.

"Am I being too up-front with this?" she thought. "Maybe I should suggest meeting in some café in the village, instead of here. Maybe I shouldn't tell a man about Alice until we've been out a few times and had a chance to connect. But that's deceptive. Anyway I don't have *time* for it! I need a husband *soon!* Should I reword the ad?"

Desperately seeking husband and father.

Like, this week.

The thoughts in her head raced on like a roller coaster, fast and frightening on their well-worn track.

"Because if I'm not married, if there's no husband in the picture, then Dr. Feldman is going to recom-

mend to the family court that custody of Alice goes
to Mom. And Dr. Feldman's recommendation will
count more than anything else, because of what Jodie
said about his guardianship in the will she made at
the beginning of her pregnancy.''

Jodie hadn't even known about Suzanne's existence at that point.

''And Mom can't have Alice, because that baby
needs love, and Mom doesn't know how to love anyone but herself, no matter how well she can pretend.
I have the love. I love that baby so much! It's changed
all my plans, changed my future completely. But
where am I going to find a man, *soon,* who can care
about her the way I do?''

Suzanne didn't have any answers, and she didn't
have any more potential husbands to meet today. She
crammed the deal-breaking, heartbreaking little pink
bootie back in her purse, took a final gulp of her sixth
or seventh coffee and headed for the elevator. For the
moment, finding a man to fit the bootie—a prince of
a man, with a hero's heart—would have to wait. She
wanted to get back to the neonatal unit to see her baby
girl.

''Alice has a visitor already, Suzanne,'' said Terri
McAllister, the head nurse for this shift.

''Oh, Mom's here?'' Suzanne didn't succeed at the
upbeat tone she was trying for. Things were tense
between her and Mom at the moment. There could
easily be a custody battle between them, but she
didn't want people knowing this. Not even the nurses
here, who had been so wonderful since Alice's birth.

''Uh, no, it's not your mother,'' Terri said. ''I don't

think she's been in here for about ten days.'' Her tone dropped sympathetically. ''She told me it's so difficult for her to get here, what with all her charity work in Philadelphia.''

Yeah, Mom's very believable when she says things like that.

''So who—?'' Suzanne said aloud.

''This is someone new.'' Something in the way Terri spoke sent a prickle of warning up Suzanne's spine. ''His name is Stephen Serkin, and he had a letter of introduction from Dr. Feldman. He's only been in the country a couple of days, I think.''

''What on earth…?''

Suzanne didn't finish. Easing past Terri, she could see the whole unit. It was brightly lit and crowded with the complex equipment needed for the care of ill or premature newborns. Her eyes skimmed over other babies, other visitors, and went instinctively to the far end, where Alice's Plexiglas crib was positioned.

The crib hadn't always been that far along in the unit. For more than two months, Alice was in the room beside the nurses' station that was reserved for the most fragile babies of all. Moving to the far end was a ''graduation'' that Suzanne valued much more than her own graduation from college, complete with cap and gown and a degree in library science.

Today, there was a man sitting in the hard beige plastic chair on the far side of Alice's crib—the chair where Suzanne herself had spent so many hours. He was watching the sleeping baby intently, and hadn't yet looked up at Suzanne's approach. She was walking carefully, and maybe he hadn't heard.

She took advantage of this, and paused to watch him. Still didn't have any idea who he was, or why he was here. Stephen Serkin. The name didn't ring a bell. Despite the letter of introduction, which Dr. Feldman had apparently written on the man's behalf, Feldman hadn't mentioned any Stephen Serkin to her. And she had never seen him before in her life.

She would have remembered a man like this.

He was wearing blue denim jeans and a white T-shirt, and there was a brown leather jacket hanging over the back of the chair. The temperature in the unit was kept high for the sake of the babies, so he didn't need the jacket in here. The garment looked well-worn, and must hug his body snugly when he had it on. Those shoulders, beneath the T-shirt, were broad and strong, and so was his chest.

He seemed to be consumed by his thoughts, although his eyes were fixed on baby Alice. They were very blue eyes, the color of shadows on snow, and above them was a frown. A lot of people frowned when they saw Alice for the first time. She was still so tiny, and still wore an oxygen mask. This stranger seemed to be measuring her in his mind, and as Suzanne watched, he bent a little closer, as if he needed to study the baby more closely still.

The movement brought his hair into the light. It was a rich, glossy brown, just long enough to fall into a couple of loose waves across the top of his well-shaped head, and it gleamed with strands of gold.

He had a scar down one cheek, Suzanne noticed as she came closer. Nothing dramatic. Just a silvery white line. It gave him an exotic look. Her gaze traveled along the thin line to reach his mouth and she saw that his top lip was just a little fuller than the lower one.

My lord, who could he be? she wondered again.

A little sound of apprehension and dismay escaped from her throat as she came past the crib next to Alice's. It caught his attention at last. He looked up. Their eyes met, and Suzanne saw a flash of interest and anticipation in those blue eyes. Neither of them smiled. For a stretched out moment, neither of them even spoke.

Suzanne felt his assessment of her like the hot glare of a surgical lamp. She flushed. What was he thinking? There was a calculation in his regard, as if they were two athletes about to go head to head in a race.

"You must be Suzanne," he said at last. "Is that right? Josephine's half sister?"

"I'm Jodie's half sister, yes."

She used her dead sister's nickname deliberately, as if to underline their connection and the fact that it was stronger than any connection he could possibly claim. *No one* had called Jodie Rimsky "Josephine." Even her listing under Physicians in the Manhattan telephone directory had read, "Jodie Rimsky, M.D."

"But I have no idea about you," she added. His English was fluent and attractive to the ear, but there was an accent, most noticeable when he had said Jodie's name. Terri had said he'd only been in the country for a couple of days. Was he French?

"I'm her first cousin. *Jodie's* first cousin." He emphasized the nickname as if to admit that Suzanne had won that particular point. The cynical little tuck at the corner of his mouth suggested it would be her last victory. "Our fathers were brothers."

Shocked, Suzanne seized on one tiny fact that didn't make sense. It was like pulling on a tail of yarn in the hope that the whole sweater would unravel. For some reason, she instinctively wanted this man's story, whatever it was, to unravel *now*. Dr. Feldman had mentioned to her in passing that Jodie had some relatives in Europe, but he hadn't made it sound all that important. Why was this man here, seated beside Alice's crib? He'd come such a long way.

"If your fathers were brothers, then your name should be Rimsky," she said. "But Terri said it was Serkin."

"More properly…or historically…it's Serkin-Rimsky," he explained, his face still unsmiling. "Our fathers chose to simplify it in different ways. My passport still says Serkin, but I'll be using the Serkin-Rimsky name in full from now on."

It sounded like a threat.

"What do you want?" Suzanne asked, her voice harsh with apprehension.

Her gut was churning like a washing machine. It shouldn't be like this! Most probably, he didn't want anything. But she was so used to people *wanting* or *not wanting* Alice, she could only think of it in such terms now.

Mom and her new husband, Perry, *wanted* Alice. They wanted the wealth held in trust for her, through the terms of Jodie's will. They *didn't want* the health problems that were sometimes associated with premature birth. Their interest in the tiny child had only developed after the reading of Jodie's will, and after Alice's health had begun to improve.

Dr. Feldman, Alice's temporary guardian, *wanted*

the baby to go to a close blood relative who could make a stable, two-parent family for her. He *didn't want* her to go to Suzanne. "Although I have a lot of sympathy for your position," he'd said.

Unfortunately, however, Suzanne wasn't married, she was only the baby's half aunt, and she was just camped out in an echoing, unrenovated loft apartment, a short-term, four-month rental here in New York City. She hadn't had time to settle in. She spent all her time at the hospital or at her financially necessary part-time library job.

Finally, all those men she'd met through the personal ad *didn't want* to get saddled with a premature adopted newborn, at the very beginning of a new relationship. They didn't want a lukewarm marriage of convenience in order to provide Suzanne with an instant husband. Oh, and she couldn't blame them for that. It had been a crazy idea to advertise, but she was so desperate, so single-minded about it now.

Suzanne felt as if she were the only person in the world who thought about Alice in terms of love instead of wanting. She'd loved Alice, welcomed her into her heart and her life, from the moment she'd laid eyes on her in early July. Back then, Alice had weighed less than two pounds. No one could be sure she'd even survive. Back then, Suzanne had had no idea that the baby had inherited wealth, or that Dr. Feldman would prove so firm on the subject of stability and marriage.

"What do I *want?*" Stephen Serkin repeated.

"Yes." She glared at him. "I mean, are you going to tell me you've come all the way from...?" She paused, and left him to fill in the blank.

"From Europe. From Aragovia," he answered.

"From Europe," she repeated. Hadn't heard of Aragovia. "…to bring her a teddy bear, or something?"

"Not a teddy bear."

For the first time, he smiled. His teeth were very white, but a little crooked at the top, on one side of his mouth, near the silver line of his scar. It made his smile just a bit uneven. And somehow softer, less intimidating, Suzanne decided with reluctance. Along with the glint of humor in those astonishing blue eyes, it invited others to share in his pleasure. She watched as he leaned down to the floor and pulled something from a shopping bag.

"I've brought her a doll," he said.

"Oh."

"Is that all right?" He held it out for her to inspect, as if her opinion mattered. She took it, not knowing what else to do. For a moment, their fingers touched.

"That's fine," she said. "Of course."

Nothing made sense. This man hadn't come to America just to give Alice a doll! Suzanne was bristling with mistrust, but she was touched by his gesture all the same.

It wasn't some mass-produced synthetic collectible, wired into position inside a clear plastic box, that he could have picked up at an airport store. It was made of cloth and yarn, with a dainty, hand-painted face, and was dressed in what looked like the national folk costume from some place in Europe.

Aragovia?

It was tragic that she knew so little about her half sister. There was a ten-year age gap between them, and Suzanne hadn't even known of Jodie's existence until last spring. They'd only met twice. The second time, Jodie had just found out that her baby would be a girl, and had confided, "I want to name her Alice. That's partly a blend of my parents' names, Alex and Lisette, but it's also after my favorite doll, as a child. She slept with me for years, until we lost her at a motel on vacation. I remember crying for so long! Memories like that come back strong when you're pregnant, I've found."

This was one of the few personal stories Suzanne had heard about her half sister's past, and they would never have a chance to know each other better now.

"She's allowed to have toys, I hope?" Stephen Serkin asked.

"Now, yes, if it's clean and new," Suzanne answered. "Her immune system is more developed than it was."

Distracted, she turned to the crib, the soft, pretty doll still in her hand. The hand-embroidered cotton skirts of the doll's dress tickled her wrist. She placed it where Alice would be able to see it. The baby had begun to focus on faces and black-and-white patterns now.

"She's waking up...." she murmured. Alice was stirring.

"No, dreaming, I think," came that complicated, musical accent. Rising to his feet, Stephen stood next to Suzanne and they both looked down at baby Alice. "Look at that! Smiling, too," he added.

"Smiling? Oh dear lord, *smiling?*" Suzanne couldn't believe it. "She's never done that before."

"But she is now, in her sleep. Look! Isn't it a great

sight?'' He laughed, a throaty sound of pure, genuine appreciation.

"I—I can't believe it. Isn't it just gas, or something?''

"It's not impossible, Suzanne," Terri McAllister interjected, having overheard. She was checking another baby in a nearby crib. "It seems like preemies should be too little to smile, when they should still be inside a tummy in the warm and dark. But actually they smile almost as early as babies who get born when they're supposed to.''

Suzanne gripped the Plexiglas sides of the crib and leaned closer. The smile came again, quite unmistakable now.

"Oh, Alice! Oh, you *are!*'' she cooed.

The smile was wider this time. It was an open-mouthed and completely toothless beam that scooped dimples into each cheek and softened the baby's whole face, even in sleep. She stretched and arched her little neck. Her creamy eyelids still seemed almost transparent, their skin was so fine.

"What on earth can she be dreaming about that's making her so delighted and happy?'' Suzanne wondered aloud.

"You,'' Stephen said. He was still standing beside her, and Suzanne felt the warmth of his forearm against her wrist. His hip bumped her side.

"Me?'' she echoed.

She was trying desperately not to be so conscious of his accidental touch. Out of the corner of her eye she could see just how well made his arms were. They were strong and smooth, with lengths of honed muscle. He must keep himself fit.

"Yes, you." He smiled at her for the second time. "Of course, you."

This time, she noticed the way the smile crinkled the skin around his eyes and lit up his whole face. Like Alice's smile. Again, there was a teasing quality to it that immediately made her smile back. Slowly she was beginning to lose that instinctive mistrust. Maybe here, at last, was someone else who didn't just think about *wants*. Alice was his cousin's child. Was it possible that he actually cared?

"She's dreaming about your voice," he continued. "Your fragrance. The songs you sing to her."

They were both watching the baby again, intent on every tiny movement in her face, every eyelid flicker and every wobble of her little fists.

"How did you know I sing to her?" Suzanne asked.

"Of course you sing! I've heard so many mothers singing to their babies in hospital at home in Aragovia. I'm a family doctor, myself."

Suzanne felt a sudden twist in her gut, and a shock of recognition. "Jodie was a pediatrician." She blinked back tears.

"I know. I did my family practice residency here in the United States, when she had just completed her specialist training. We were quite good friends for a while."

"I got the impression most people liked her." She was still struggling, didn't really know what she was saying. Why had his tone changed, on that last sentence? She had so many unanswered questions about the man, this one seemed too trivial to think about.

"It distresses you to talk about your sister," he

said. He'd noticed her face and her swimming eyes. "We won't do it now."

"You mean…?"

"At some point soon, we need to. For now, let's watch Alice's smile."

He turned back to the baby and began a lullaby in a language she didn't recognize, singing so softly that she could hardly hear it. The tune was poignantly beautiful, and there was a tiny catch in his voice on certain notes. Suzanne could almost feel the way the melody tugged at her heart. Did Stephen Serkin know what a gorgeous voice he had?

Of course he did. A confident man didn't reach his thirties without knowing exactly which of his attributes and talents most appealed to women. She had the sudden instinct that there was something too deliberate about this, something that didn't ring true.

She reacted against the emotion that had momentarily blinded her. Stepping away from him, she said in a cold tone, "You still haven't told me why you're here."

"It's not such a mystery, is it?" he answered. "I had a business matter to attend to in New York, and I wanted to see my cousin's child."

"Then you already knew about Jodie's death?"

"Yes."

"Dr. Feldman contacted you? He went through all the names in Jodie's address book."

"I expect that's how he reached me. I didn't actually ask."

"Then you've—?"

"I saw him yesterday, and he arranged for me to be able to visit here."

"How long will you be in New York?"

"That depends. I'll stay as long as I need to. It might be weeks. Longer." He paused for a moment. "You seem suspicious about all this. About me. Why is that?"

Suzanne controlled a sigh and her mind raced as she sorted through what she felt safe in telling him, and what she didn't want to reveal. She didn't dare to look at him.

"Alice's future is…so uncertain at the moment," she said, still staring down at the tiny baby.

She was dressed only in a diaper as small and thin as an envelope, a white undershirt patterned with pastel rocking horses and little pink booties. She still had a feed tube in her nose, an oxygen mask on her face and monitors all over.

"It's no secret that I'd like to get custody and bring her up as my own," she added.

"Yes, so I understand."

"I've been here every single day since she was born, and I love her so much. But that doesn't mean I'll be able to keep her permanently."

"I know." His voice had softened. "There's your mother's claim, too."

"You *know?*"

"I talked with Michael Feldman for a while. I wanted to find out as much as I could. Look, we can't have this discussion here. It's too important, and there's so much we have to work out."

"Work out?" She was really alarmed, now. "What do we have to work out?"

Her head whirled around toward him too fast, and

she swayed unsteadily for a moment. The neonatal unit went dark, then her vision cleared again.

"Are you all right?" His fingers brushed a strand of hair away from her mouth, and he was frowning.

"I'm fine." She shook her hair back, not wanting his hand anywhere near her face. "I felt a little light-headed for a moment, that's all."

"How have you been sleeping lately?"

"Not very well," she admitted. "I'm here every day, and I have to try to slot it in around work. I've got a lot to think about. And then I've had—" she counted remorsefully "—seven cups of coffee today." With all those men who weren't interested in fitting little pink booties into their lives. "I don't usually do that."

"You're under a lot of strain," he said. "There are things you haven't told me, yet."

"You think so?"

"And things I haven't told you. As I said before, we need to work it all out, and it looks to me as if you need to eat, instead of drinking seven cups of coffee."

"What are you suggesting?"

"There's a coffee shop just off the lobby."

"Believe me, I know it!"

She must have eaten a hundred meals there over the past couple of months. Didn't suggest going elsewhere, because there didn't seem much point. She didn't want to turn this "talk" of his into a big production.

So this was why, five minutes later, there she was at her favorite table near the window—the one where she'd met Robert and Les and Colin and Dan—waiting for her burger, fries and soda to arrive and rummaging frantically in her messy purse for her packet of tissues. The woman sitting behind her had cat hair on her jacket, and Suzanne was allergic, and—

"Ah-ah-choo!" She got the tissue to her nose just in time, grabbed at another one and saw that familiar little pink bootie drop out onto the table. Not surprising. It had been deliberately positioned right on top of the clutter that filled her purse.

Sneezing for the third time, she thought, I'm sick of the sight of that bootie, now. It hasn't helped.

Stephen picked the bootie up and fiddled with it absently, the way he might have fiddled with a pencil on a desk.

This isn't where I want to be, he thought. *This isn't how I'd be handling the situation if there was more time, or if this woman wasn't involved. I don't enjoy playing a double game. But I can't see any choice. My country must come first. My father taught me that, and my great-grandmother....*

He was tired, he knew. His emotions had been buffeted by all the changes that had come in his life over the past few months, and the ones that were still ahead. Most of those changes were good. The Aragovian people had voted for a new constitution, with the heir to the Serkin-Rimsky family's ancestral throne as the nation's head of state. He had enormous hopes for his life and his country, now—hopes that would have seemed almost impossible to realize sixteen years ago, when he'd reached legal adulthood at eighteen.

But he wasn't safe yet. Nothing was set in stone

yet. Not in his country and not, it now appeared, in tiny Alice's life. He was under pressure from his political advisers at home. Pressure to ensure that the line of succession was rock solid, by whatever means necessary. Pressure to marry as soon as possible. A suitable bride. Someone the Aragovian people would come to love. Her actual identity hardly mattered, let alone Stephen's feelings for her.

"As a bachelor prince, Stephen, you are vulnerable to unsuitable women from your past with an eye on what you have to offer now."

"Unsuitable women? Well, yes, there have been one or two of those...."

"No one now?"

"No."

His last meaningful relationship had been with an American woman, part of the same family practice residency program as himself. Elin would have been "suitable." Like Jodie, however, she hadn't wanted him to return to Aragovia, and they'd parted in mutual anger. He'd heard she was now married to someone else.

Since then, his work as a doctor and the changing situation in his country had kept him too busy to think of relationships, suitable or otherwise.

And then there was baby Alice's situation. He had talked with Feldman for a long time, yesterday.

"Jodie talked about you," Michael Feldman had said, with a reserve that Stephen hadn't missed. "She didn't want anything to do with you at one stage, and certainly nothing to do with a place as obscure as Aragovia. Her father never believed there was any future for your family there."

"No. That's why he left, in the fifties. My father felt differently."

"What's the situation there now? The place is controlled by Russian mafia, isn't it?"

"It was. Or by a couple of offshoots of it. But that's changed now. There is high hope for the future of the country."

"You should be thinking of *your* future, and just get out."

Stephen hadn't known how to answer that. He had earned a great deal of respect in his country over the past few years, through his medical work there. He had almost lost his life in defense of its heritage, and he had firm hope that his devotion to Aragovia would soon be rewarded. He wasn't planning to "just get out."

And yet Dr. Feldman was right about Jodie and her attitude. Stephen's friendship with his cousin had soured, in the end, as a result of their sharply diverging views. Should he admit any of this to Suzanne? Should he tell her the full truth?

No, not yet. Definitely not yet.

His talk with Michael Feldman had continued in a more instructive vein. He'd learned about Suzanne and her claim on Alice. He'd learned about Suzanne's mother, Rose, too. Feldman had told him that, as the child's grandmother, her claim was stronger.

And he had begun to perceive a strategy, one which would please his advisers on all fronts.

It wasn't the first Stephen had heard of Rose Chaloner Brown Wigan, nee Norton. His father's brother, Alex Rimsky, had confided in him, some years ago, in a way that some men would only confide in a male relative.

"Jodie is my biological daughter, Stepan." His accent was thick even after more than thirty years in the United States, and he used the Russian form of Stephen's name. "She was the—how should I put it?—*product* of a brief and regrettable liaison just before I met Lisette. Jodie doesn't know it. We told her from the beginning that she was adopted, and that is also true."

"Complicated!"

"Not really. The adoption was conducted through official channels, when her natural mother gave her up at birth. You see, Lisette knew that she was unable to bear a child of her own. There was an operation for medical reasons years before. And Rose Norton did not want a child."

"That sounds very cold."

Alex had shrugged. "She was young and beautiful and selfish, and she had big plans for her life. Devil knows if she ever attained her dreams! They were so unrealistic. But then, who knew that I would have such success? Certainly, Rose did not believe it possible. She saw me as a poor, futureless immigrant, who had briefly captured her sensuality. I have no idea what became of her."

And Alex Rimsky had died last year, without ever learning more about Rose, just a few months after the death of Lisette.

The deaths of her parents had affected Jodie deeply, Michael Feldman had told Stephen yesterday. During his final illness, Alex had told his daughter the truth about her origins. This had set her on a quest to find her birth mother. She had also become desperate to have a child of her own, although she was single, and had chosen artificial insemination through a reputable clinic.

A strong-willed, charismatic woman, Jodie had succeeded in both goals—becoming pregnant and finding Rose. This was when she'd learned she had two younger half sisters, through the first of Rose's three marriages. The elder of those sisters was the woman who sat opposite Stephen now, thanking the waitress politely as their order arrived.

He liked her already. She wasn't beautiful, but she had a presence about her—a quiet glow that was more attractive to his eye than shallow, model-perfect looks. Those green eyes were so warm and bright against her fair skin.

Her medium-dark hair waved so softly against her cheeks. It was a little untidy at this stage of the day, betraying the fact that she had a lot of other things on her mind. Her clothes were neat and pretty, though—tailored pale gray pants, a short-sleeved cream knit top and a delicate little necklace made of tiny beads and stones. The figure beneath the clothes was, on his closer inspection, more lushly curved than he had realized at first.

Her full, sensitive mouth seemed to draw his gaze, and she had a faint sprinkling of tiny golden freckles on her nose. The determined jaw told him that he shouldn't underestimate her because of this youthful look. She wasn't a woman he'd be able to manipulate at will. He was going to have to handle it carefully.

Her love for baby Alice was obvious. It was shaded into the glow of her eyes, sketched into the shape of her mouth. It captivated him and confirmed that he was on the right track in what he planned to do. First and foremost, beyond any question of politics and destiny, a baby like Alice needed love.

"Suzanne Brown is itching to adopt Jodie's baby," Dr. Feldman had said. "And it's clear that she cares. But she's being unrealistic. She's not the child's closest blood relative, and her circumstances are precarious at this stage. She's not married, not involved with anyone, and I believe very strongly in two-parent families."

"Yes, I can understand that."

"I was never in favor of what Jodie was doing, setting out to have a baby on her own. Perhaps I should have told her my views on that more clearly. At that stage, though, I thought it wasn't my concern. It is now!"

He had finished with a helpless shake of his head.

Stephen had said little in response. He wasn't yet prepared to reveal his agenda to anyone. Feldman didn't seem to believe in the future that Stephen hoped for.

Maybe no one here believed that it would really happen.

Stephen did, and he would have leaped to resume his title and the throne, as his people wanted. The only problem was, he wasn't the rightful heir...

He picked up a French fry and slid it into his mouth, barely tasting the salt or the crisp heat. Food seemed irrelevant at the moment. He flicked the little pink bootie in his left hand from one finger to the other and let it finally come to rest on his thumb. The thing was so tiny that it fitted there perfectly.

There was no point in hesitating any longer. Suzanne was halfway through her burger and she was watching him with her huge green eyes, waiting to hear what he had to say.

"I have a proposition for you, Suzanne," he said slowly. "We both have Alice's best interests at heart. Am I right in thinking you would give almost anything to be able to bring her up as your own?"

"Of course I would," she answered. "I love her. It's the only thing I want, right now."

"Then I think we should get married."

Chapter Two

"I don't understand why you'd be willing to do this," Suzanne said, several confused minutes later. She took a gulp of her soda in an attempt to refresh her dry mouth.

Stephen's offer had seriously spooked her. It clearly wasn't something he'd come up with on the spur of the moment. He'd been thinking about it. For how long, she didn't know. Since his meeting with Dr. Feldman?

She had been hunting down a husband for nearly two months. She'd called up two former boyfriends, but it hadn't taken long to cross those names off her list. They had been clumsy, lackluster relationships in the first place, and the passage of several years hadn't helped.

She'd made some discreet inquiries through friends. Any men out there with a reason of their own for wanting to sprint down the aisle at short notice? No takers. She'd placed that ill-fated personal ad.

Now, this stranger, Jodie's first cousin, had offered her just what she wanted and she was holding back, wary and skeptical.

"Does that matter?" he asked. "Do my reasons matter?"

"Of course they matter!" She crashed her soda glass onto the table, splashing her hand with cold, fizzy liquid. "Obviously it would help my case if we got married, and you've realized that, but what do you stand to gain from it?"

"The same thing that you do, Suzanne." He was watching her, his eyes steady and open. "The knowledge that it will give Alice the best chance of a happy future."

"My mother and her husband, Perry, are planning to give her exactly that. It's not as if she's going to get sent to an orphanage, or something. She'll have a mom and a dad and it'll be fine."

"If that's the case, why are you fighting it?" he asked.

She couldn't answer. Just sat there with her mouth half-open, feeling as if someone had doused her in a bucket of hot water. He had cut to the heart of the issue in nine words. If she could sincerely believe that Mom and Perry would love Alice and would put her first in their lives, then she wouldn't be scrambling so desperately for ways to strengthen her claim, and Stephen Serkin-Rimsky knew it.

So maybe he did care. He'd talked to Michael Feldman, and he wasn't stupid. He understood the situation, and he cared.

"Where would we live?" she asked.

He blinked. "Well...wherever is best for Alice."

"Okay...I'll have more questions."

She meant it as a threat, but he only laughed. "I don't promise I'll have the answers to all of them."

"I—I need to think about this," she told him. The blood was still beating in her head. To occupy her nervous hands, she began soaking up the little puddles of spilled soda with the corner of a napkin.

"I didn't demand an instant decision, did I?" One corner of that firm mouth lifted again.

"No, but if it's going to happen, it has to happen soon," she retorted, lightning fast.

Then she saw the flare of satisfaction in his blue eyes, like the flare of a match striking. He could almost *touch* the intensity of her need, she realized. It wasn't a position of strength, on her part.

"Yes, it does," he agreed. "But we can take a few days to think about what's involved, about what it means. The implications of a divorce, if that became necessary sometime in the future. The question of how far we are prepared to go, how much of ourselves we are prepared to give, in order to make it real."

He didn't mention the word *sex,* but perhaps he didn't need to. They both knew it was what he meant. She wondered if the prospect should shock her, and immediately discovered that it didn't. Yes, she could—theoretically, abstractly, distantly—imagine sleeping with him. Despite the distance and the abstraction, it was unsettling. She didn't often respond physically to a man within an hour of their first meeting.

"I really need to think about this," she repeated.

"Do you think that I don't?" he said. His smile was crooked, inviting hers in return. "Do you think that I've answered all these questions for myself? I haven't! I'll give you the phone number of my hotel. Call me whenever you want to. I'll take your number, too. We might both have things to talk about.''

Suzanne nodded slowly. "That makes sense.''

She felt like adding, "I'm going to see Dr. Feldman, too. Check you out a little further.''

As long as she could manage to do that without giving away too much herself. She didn't want Michael to guess that she was contemplating a strategic marriage to Jodie's cousin. She'd prefer to present it to him as a done deal after the event, a practical yet optimistic arrangement that was already working well.

"Finish your burger," Stephen said. "Will it help Alice if you get sick?"

"No, I guess it won't,'' she agreed, and picked up the half-cooled burger. Duty, not pleasure.

He watched, wearing a small, satisfied smile, and when she had finished eating, he flicked the little bootie back to her, across the table. "Don't forget this," he said.

"It fits your thumb better than it fits her foot, now," she answered him. "She's grown so much since she was born.''

"May I keep it, then?"

"For your thumb? Gloves would be a little more useful.''

He laughed. "No, not for my thumb. I'll send it to my mother, at home, so she can see how frighteningly tiny Alice must have been when she was born. She will probably cry at the sight of it." His face had fallen into serious lines once more. "She would have come here with me, to see the baby, only she's been ill. She had some major surgery a couple of weeks ago.''

''Oh, I'm sorry to hear that.''

''The discovery of this baby has done wonders for her recovery. I know she'll want all the news of Alice that I can give her.''

And that was the moment when I knew, Suzanne thought to herself several days later. When he said that, I knew that he really did care about Alice, and I knew, for better or for worse, no matter what we decided about sex and divorce, that I'd marry him....

Rose Norton Chaloner Brown Wigan had never stayed at a five-star New York hotel before, but she was trying very hard to act as if she stayed in such establishments all the time.

It was quite sweet, in a way. At the strangest times, Suzanne detected an odd form of innocence in her selfish, beautiful and eternally blond mother. Rose and Perry had arrived from Philadelphia two days ago, ''Now that our commitments have allowed us to get back here again, for a longer stay, we're itching to see that darling baby!''

Their commitments had allowed them to do this for about two hours yesterday morning, just before lunch at Tavern on the Green.

They planned to stay over the weekend, and Mom had begged Suzanne over the phone, with that same exultant innocence, ''You must come and see our suite, honey! It's spectacular!''

Dropping in to visit Rose, as promised, Suzanne was greeted with the eager offer of anything she liked from the minibar of the sixth floor park view room.

Just absolutely anything at all. A cocktail? Champagne? Chocolates?

"No, I'm fine, thanks." Tense, too. She had something to discuss, and knew that the mood would change, at that point, like fall weather coming down from Canada on the tail end of a steamy summer.

"Are you sure, darling?" Rose said. "If there's something you want that isn't here, I can order it in special."

"I'm really not hungry or thirsty." She added gently, "You know they charge a bundle for all these little drinks and candies, Mom." She didn't want her mother to get carried away. Maybe Mom thought that you got these things for free. She and Perry could end up with an appalling bar bill, on top of what had to be a mammoth tab for this suite.

But Rose didn't seem to care. "We're putting it all on credit cards," she said. "It's not a problem, Suzie, really it isn't, because we'll pay them off no trouble, as soon as all the legal stuff with Alice's inheritance goes through."

Rose couldn't quite keep the glee out of her face, but tried a little harder when her sideways glance caught Suzanne's frown.

"I mean, as Alice's new parents," she continued in an earnest tone, as if giving a public speech, "we can't be expected to live like—like hillbillies, can we?"

"No, Mom. I can't see you as a hillbilly, I admit."

"She's an heiress, and we need to start moving amongst the right people—society people, you know, people who stay in hotels like this all the time—so she can make the right contacts. Perry and I have

talked about this very seriously, and we both agree
it's the right thing.''

"I'm glad you've got your priorities worked out,
Mom," Suzanne said. Only someone who knew her
very well would have picked the subtle flavor of sarcasm in her mild tone. Rose wasn't that someone.

"Well, yes," she answered. "Perry and I both
know how important it is.''

She glanced toward her husband, who was
stretched out on the couch, sleeping the way an alli-
gator sleeps in a nice, warm Florida swamp—decep-
tively.

Suzanne wished she could count on his nap being
genuine. She had that weather-changing announce-
ment for Mom, and wanted to be able to make it
without his input.

She took a deep breath, instead, before she spoke.
"I have some news, Mom, which I hope you'll be
pleased about.''

"News? What news?" Having picked up something significant in her daughter's tone, Rose attempted to narrow her eyes.

This was difficult. The face-lift surgery she'd had
several months ago had pulled her skin so tight she
wore a perpetual look of attractive, wide-eyed surprise. But the intent to narrow them was definitely
there, Suzanne decided.

She bit the bullet.

"I'm getting married on Friday, and I want both
of you to come to the wedding.'' As Rose had done
a moment earlier, Suzanne glanced at Perry, but he
hadn't stirred.

"Getting married on—! But that's the day after tomorrow!'' Rose paced the room like a soap opera actress. Her mouth was set in a line of concentration, and she was obviously thinking hard. She spun around on the high navy heels that matched her imitation silk suit, and as Suzanne had expected, the drop in temperature had arrived.

"I know why you're doing this," Rose accused suddenly.

"You haven't asked me who he is." Suzanne plowed on, as if she hadn't heard.

Getting her head down, getting stubborn and pretending a sudden hearing loss was the only way she could deal successfully with her mother.

"It's because of that baby. And Feldman's views on stability and two-parent families," Rose said, ignoring Suzanne just as thoroughly. "I thought you'd given up on this stupid rift you're so determined to make between us, Suzie!"

"I'm not making a rift." I'm not going to let her get to me.

"I've told you, it doesn't need to be like this. Do you think I'd stop you from seeing the child?"

"His name is Stephen Serkin."

"It won't work, darling." She sat down beside her daughter and put a soft, cajoling hand on her knee. Her eyes were swimming with sudden tears. "Look, you know I love you." Her voice cracked. "You're my daughter. This isn't a battle, and it hurts me that you're starting to treat it like one. Alice should come to me. I'm her closest blood relative. Accept it."

"He's thirty-four years old, and a doctor," Suzanne stated. "Specializing in family practice. And he's Jodie's first cousin."

Crisp fall weather gave way to Arctic winter.

"What?" Rose hissed. "So this is a total conspiracy! You think that a half aunt and a first cousin once removed add up to more than a grandmother?"

"It's not a question of *adding up*."

Again, Rose ignored her. "You're wrong! How did you track him down, anyway?"

"I didn't track him down. He came from Europe to visit Alice."

"Oh, from *Europe?* To visit a *baby?* An ugly little thing who doesn't even know she's alive? Trust me, there's more to it than that!"

"She's smiled at me three days in a row."

"Honey, that's gas," Rose snapped, apparently reaching the end of her rope.

Suzanne remained as calm as she could—on the surface, at least.

"He and Jodie knew each other quite well at one time," she said, returning to what was relevant. "He studied medicine, here in New York. Jodie would have been pleased about our decision."

The conviction in her voice was genuine.

She and Stephen had talked on the phone several times since their first meeting nine days ago, and had talked for long stretches beside Alice's crib as well. They had gone to city hall to get their marriage license yesterday, and to a jewelry store to pick two simple gold wedding bands. The errands hadn't taken long. Less than two hours. And the impending marriage still didn't seem quite real. But during all of this they'd started to get to know each other a little.

Stephen had retained the instinctive courtesy she'd seen in him last week, and the same humor and care.

As for those two big questions, sex and divorce, "We'll know, when either becomes appropriate, I think!" he'd said, with the upside-down smile she was starting to know.

Suzanne's liking and trust had grown, building on her vivid image of him mailing a tiny pink bootie home to his convalescent mother in Aragovia. That was a gesture that couldn't have been faked, surely!

"Did your mom get the bootie yet?" she had asked him yesterday.

"Yes, she called me last night. She was relieved to hear it was way too small for Alice now, and she's started knitting bigger booties. Hats and sweaters and mittens, too, I expect. All pink. She loves pink. Be prepared to receive large, soft parcels with foreign stamps."

Suzanne had laughed. She was becoming more and more certain that she'd been wrong about her initial moments of doubt and mistrust.

And Dr. Feldman had confirmed that Stephen was genuine.

"I had a diplomat friend check it out for me," he had told Suzanne. "Anyone could blow in claiming to be Jodie's Aragovian cousin, after all. But he's exactly who he says he is, although I admit, I'm not yet convinced about the latest developments in his home country."

"Developments?"

"I tend to discount the whole Aragovian thing. Jodie always did. She mentioned her cousin to me several times. I wouldn't be surprised if he ends up making a permanent home here."

"Oh, really?" She'd tried not to let her face light

up. That would certainly help. She wasn't sure what Dr. Feldman had meant by "the whole Aragovian thing," but it didn't matter, surely, if there was a good chance that Stephen was planning to remain here.

"Why wouldn't he?" Dr. Feldman had said. "He's qualified to practice medicine here, and he has the good example of his uncle to follow. Jodie's father made a fortune in the U.S. after starting out as an immigrant without two pennies to rub together."

Stephen had asked, this morning, if he could meet her somewhere on Friday afternoon, shortly before the ceremony. He had something for her, he'd said. She wondered what it could be. Hadn't wanted to ask, and he hadn't given any clues. He'd just said it.

"Something for you. For the wedding. And we might need to talk a little."

They hadn't been able to think of a place to meet, and had finally settled on simply arriving at the church an hour before the ceremony. It wasn't one of Manhattan's fashionable Fifth Avenue churches, but a little place in an out-of-the-way corner of Chelsea, where an old friend of Suzanne's late and much loved stepfather still presided. John Davenport had happily agreed to perform the ceremony, as long as they could squeeze it in at three o'clock.

So Suzanne was meeting Stephen there at two, less than forty-eight hours away. She already felt a warm lick of anticipation curling inside her. Anticipation, and desperation.

"Jodie would have been pleased about your decision?" Rose was repeating in a derisory tone. "What do you know about Jodie? She was *my* daughter."

"You gave her up for adoption at birth."

"Because I was young, and alone, and penniless! It was more than thirty-seven years ago. Girls didn't keep their illegitimate babies then. Not unless they were fools."

"When she made contact with you this year, you didn't want to know her."

"What was the point? What good would it have done? To drag up that whole affair?" Suddenly, she gave a cynical laugh, and her focus seemed to fix on something in her mind's eye. "Well, at least, in hindsight, if I'd known that Alex Rimsky had done so well for himself, I might have been able to get something out of it. Heaven knows, I deserve some security, don't I? After all I've had to deal with in my life!" She blinked back tears. "But never mind that. We're talking about your *marriage*." Rose gave the word a sour, mocking intonation.

"No, Mom, I've said all I have to say."

There was no point in prolonging this. Rose was very good at hijacking a conversation and pulling it, without warning, in exactly the direction that suited her. Suzanne didn't have that sort of cunning. All she had was love, faith and need.

She stood up, not wanting to linger until Perry woke up. "The ceremony is at three o'clock. At John Davenport's church. You remember, Dad's friend? And you remember where it is?"

"Of course! But, lord, is old John still alive, after all these years?"

"He's only in his late sixties. And, as I said, you and Perry are most welcome to come. There won't be any written invitations, obviously. And there won't be anyone else there."

"Not your sisters? Not that ghastly old cousin of Catrina's with the strange name?"

"It's Pixie. Short for Priscilla." Resisting the urge to defend her stepsister Cat's eccentric but loving cousin, Suzanne added, "No, I haven't asked them."

Suzanne had seen Cat just last week, when Cat had come up from Philadelphia for the day to see Alice. She could have asked her to the wedding. Should have. Cat and Pixie would be hurt. Jill would have been hurt, too, only she was away in Montana, supposedly organizing a divorce.

Why hadn't she asked them? She didn't want to think about the possible reasons right now, just knew she'd felt a deep-seated reluctance to get them involved.

She expected an attack from Mom, but Rose just did that strange eye narrowing thing with her face again and said, "Hmm."

"Biding her time. That's what she's doing," Suzanne thought. "Waiting until she's worked out a strategy, and talked it over with Perry."

He had just rolled over on the couch.

I shouldn't have invited her. I wanted to give her fair warning that I wasn't going to simply accept Dr. Feldman's verdict and let Alice go. But maybe that's going to backfire. There's been no chance to really think this through. What if everything I'm planning turns out to be a huge mistake?

Chapter Three

"Suzanne?"

She whirled around. "Stephen! You startled me!"

Waiting in the entrance of the chilly church, idly reading the memorial plaques on the walls, she hadn't heard him coming up the steps, and the acoustics in the dark, old building made his accented voice sound strange. The place was a little musty, smelling of aged leather, which added to the unique atmosphere.

He saw the way she had her hand fisted over her heart.

"I'm sorry," he said. "And I'm late."

"It's fine. It's not a problem," she answered, her voice not quite steady. "I was early. I came straight from the hospital."

He stepped forward and touched her arm. "How is she today? You have a little glow, as if—"

"Yes." She smiled, happy to have someone to tell. "I had a meeting with Dr. Feldman and the hospital social worker and one of the nurses. The social worker has recommended that Alice comes to me when she's first discharged, because I'm the one who is most familiar with her care.''

''That's great, Suzanne!''

''I know. And Dr. Feldman's supporting it. She'll still have the oxygen mask and the breathing alarm, and I know about those. It's only temporary, until the custody hearing, but it's a step in the right direction.''

Her teeth began to chatter with cold and nerves. ''Mom won't be happy, but she and Perry just haven't been around enough to know how to deal with the oxygen.''

''Relax!''

She shook her head. ''Can't. I've just been standing here, thinking about it all, and...''

She couldn't put it into words.

If she had been tense last week when they first met, she was doubly so today, their wedding day. She was marrying a stranger, and didn't know if he'd be coming to her apartment tonight.

Didn't know if Stephen Serkin-Rimsky had secrets, or sins. Of course! Everyone did! What were his?

''I'm sorry that you've gotten cold,'' he apologized again. ''There was a delay at the bank.'' The explanation for his lateness didn't answer any questions, just created more.

''The bank?'' Suzanne echoed.

He didn't answer. They both looked as if they'd been shopping, dressed in jeans and casual shirts, with their wedding clothes in large carrier bags. Where were the bridesmaids? The gleaming cars? The milling guests? All the usual trappings of the romantic church wedding she'd once dreamed of were missing. This was the strangest occasion, but you couldn't expect smooth-as-silk glamour and romance under such circumstances, Suzanne decided.

Lord, she wasn't going to waste precious time regretting a few details! If this arrangement increased her chance of becoming Alice's mother, that was all that mattered. She still had no idea whether Rose and Perry would even show up today, and what it would do to her chances with Alice if they did.

Could she convince them that this wedding made a difference? Could she convince Dr. Feldman?

"Are you going to dress?" Stephen asked.

"Well, I wasn't planning to get married in jeans." She heard the defensive note in her voice, and wondered why he made her feel like this. She was like a cat on hot bricks. Would have been even without the decision on Alice's temporary care.

"I meant, are you going to dress now?" he corrected himself politely, and she felt bad about how she'd overreacted to his innocent question. This couldn't be easy for him, either. They were both doing it for Alice.

"I didn't know if—" she began to explain, then changed tack. "You wanted to meet me here early. I thought you might have wanted to talk, or something. In fact you said you did, and I...thought I'd feel more comfortable talking in jeans."

"Put on your dress," he said softly. "I didn't want to talk yet. We'll have time for that in a while, and, yes, we'll need to. When you're dressed, I want to give you what I have brought."

Suzanne nodded. Why was she so breathless? She hadn't been running. It had to be nerves.

"There's a room Mr. Davenport showed me, beyond the side door at the back of the church, where there's a mirror," she answered him.

"I'll wait here," he said.

"I'll try not to take too long."

But of course she did. What woman didn't, on her wedding day?

She had bought the dress yesterday, after work. Her legs had ached from standing behind the library's front desk, and walking its stacks, reshelving books. It was a college library, not the sunny community library she would have preferred, and most of the books were thick and heavy. Standing in the mirrored fitting room at the bridal store, she hadn't felt as if she was about to get married.

In the end, she'd only tried on three dresses, and she'd chosen one based as much on its price as on its style. Having witnessed Rose openly drooling over Alice's inheritance on Wednesday, Suzanne was doubly determined not to spent a cent that she'd later "pay off with no trouble" using her baby's fortune.

Now, as she stood in front of a spotty mirror in the little room at the back of the church, the dress whispered in heavy folds of pale satin around her calves and hugged her upper body closely. She began to like it, and not just because of its price. It fit her, suited her and left plenty of room for a piece of jewelry above the elegant curve of neckline.

She had some jewelry. A necklace. Her stepfather had given it to Rose, and Rose had passed it on to

Suzanne after David Brown's death, saying, "It's dated. And it was cheap. I never liked it."

Suzanne herself had always thought that it was very pretty, a delicate design of garnets and silver. As a child, she'd often begged Rose to let her wear it, but Rose had never permitted her to do so.

Now, when she put it on, she found it didn't go with the dress. The silver looked dark and tarnished against the lustrous new satin, and the color of the stones was wrong.

It didn't matter, she decided. The sense of David Brown's love, contained in the worn piece of jewelry, was more important. But when she adjusted it on her neck, it caught in her mass of hair, and when she tried to pull it free, one of the frail links broke and the whole thing fell, useless, into her hand.

She dropped it back into its worn velvet case, and her eyes filled with tears. The necklace had brought her stepfather just a little closer. She'd almost heard his voice, almost smelled the familiar richness of the pipe tobacco he smoked.

"I should have invited Cat and Pixie," she whispered to herself. "And I should have called Jill and little Sam in Montana. At least I'd have had their smiles and their good wishes. But I was scared they'd challenge me because they'd know it wasn't real. They'd be afraid for me, that it would backfire on me, somehow."

Sex, divorce or some disaster she hadn't imagined or named.

Without her sisters she felt very alone, and remorseful that she'd shut them out. They understood how she felt about Alice. She should have trusted in their support.

And what if this wasn't her only mistake, today?

Without enthusiasm, she brushed her hair and put on her makeup. Then she found Stephen in the vestry, still wearing his jeans. He was reading the memorial plaques, just as she had done.

"Aren't you going to get dressed, too?" she asked him.

She almost hoped he'd tell her that he had changed his mind, that he couldn't go through with this. It didn't make sense, because she needed their marriage as much as she ever had. Why was she panicking like this?

"I'm sorry," he answered. "It won't take me long. But I wanted to give you these things I've brought from the bank, first. You may not want them. You need to decide. Maybe you'll want to think for a while before you do."

"I— Yes, of course," she agreed obediently, but in reality she had not a clue what was coming.

He picked up one of his carrier bags, printed with the logo of a New York department store, and pulled out two wooden boxes, one long and one square. Laid on the vestry table, both boxes gleamed like satin. They were polished to a rich sheen, inlaid with exquisite patterns of rich, dark gold timber, black ebony and iridescent mother-of-pearl.

"Both pieces are old," he explained. "Not fashionable, anymore."

"It's jewelry, then?" she asked, almost stammering. She mourned David Brown's broken necklace again in her thoughts.

"Yes, belonging to my family," Stephen answered. "I withdrew them from my bank vault today, and I will return them after the ceremony."

"They must be—"

"Valuable, yes. They are to be sold, very soon, to finance a modern hospital in Aragovia. But it is right that you should wear them, if you want to. The second Serkin-Rimsky bride to do so, and the last."

His voice was quiet and serious, and his hands moved with confident grace to unfasten the tiny metal locks on each box.

Suzanne was speechless and bewildered. He didn't look like a man who would possess jewelry of such value. She hadn't gotten the impression that he was wealthy. Doctors in central Europe didn't earn the sort of income that most American doctors did.

Her heart hammered in expectation. Inside the church, one of the wooden pews creaked. The September sun came out from behind a cloud and glowed through the stained glass on the church's west wall. The shafts of blurred, bright color stretched through the open doors and out into the vestry, lighting the place like a stage set, creating an atmosphere.

Stephen opened the smaller of the two boxes, a long rectangle. Nestled against a bed of midnight-blue velvet was a necklace of gold and diamonds that dazzled Suzanne and had her gasping with its beauty. Before she could find words, he looped it around her throat, and she felt the cold touch of the metal against her skin, as well as the ticklish heat from his careful fingers.

"There…"

"It's—it's gorgeous," was all she could say. The

gold design was as intricate as lace, and the diamonds—there had to be dozens of them—were
graded in size from tiny pinpoints of light to faceted
gems the size of a pea.

She felt his breath as he tilted his head to study the
clasp. It was just a light puff of air against her bare
collarbone, but it drew her attention to how close he
was standing, and how intently he was watching her.
She could have reached out and touched his tanned
neck, above the plain T-shirt he wore. She could have
traced the tip of her finger down the silvery line of
his scar until she reached the dented corner of his
sexy, serious mouth.

A sudden cascade of need and desire poured over
her, heating her blood and sizzling on her skin. She
could have swayed forward, then and there, to lose
herself in his arms. She could have lifted her face to
invite the touch of that mouth on hers. With everything else going on in her mind and in her heart,
though, to discover that she felt this attraction toward
him was the last thing she wanted.

Sex and divorce. If either of those things were going to happen, she'd assumed it would be some time
in a scarcely imagined future. Not now. She didn't
want to feel this now.

He was having trouble with the clasp on the necklace. "Lift your head a little," he murmured, his
shadow-blue eyes focused on the delicate oval and
gold hook. "I'm not accustomed to doing things like
this."

His fingers whispered on her skin.

She did as he'd asked, and felt him lean even
closer. His thighs dragged against the heavy satin

folds of the dress, and his forearms brushed across her breasts. He was frowning, struggling with the riddle of the clasp. She doubted that he'd noticed what an intimate, responsive part of her body his arms had touched. Prayed that he hadn't noticed, because she had noticed more than enough for both of them, and her breasts had tightened at their peaks. Her breathing quickened, and she had to fight the urge to lean even closer.

A sound of satisfaction told her that he'd succeeded at last. He slid the necklace around so that the clasp was in the middle of her nape and stepped away.

"Don't say anything yet," he told her. "Because the pieces match. They were made in Paris for my great-grandmother for her wedding, in 1912, and you must try them together before you decide."

He opened the second box, lined with the same deep-blue fabric, and touched his fingers to the circlet of gold and diamond that lay inside. She gasped.

What had she expected? A bracelet and a pair of earrings? A diamond brooch? Not this. It wasn't a crown. Crowns were for kings, and they were heavy and ornate. This was infinitely more delicate. It was a tiara, fashioned with the same dainty motifs and dazzling diamonds as the necklace, and shaped to fit a woman's head.

Stephen went to lift it up, but Suzanne shot out an angry hand and laid it across his wrists to stop him. Her treacherous, unwanted awareness of him had vanished now, thank goodness. He turned quickly away from the piece of jewelry and his startled eyes studied her, waiting, while her hand still rested on his arms.

At some level, she realized, he had expected this.

He had engineered it. He must have known she would have questions!

She found voice at last. It trembled, but it was there.

"No," she said, quite sharply. She pulled her hand away. "Don't. Not yet. Explain first. I don't understand. You're staying at a cheap, tourist hotel near Penn Station. Your clothes could have come from a discount store, and they're not new. But these jewels are priceless, you tell me, enough to finance a whole hospital. They look like things that would belong to a—"

"A princess," he finished for her. "Yes. A princess of the Aragovian royal house of Serkin-Rimsky. I could tell that you didn't know. You need to, before we go through with this. Jodie had turned her back on her heritage, as her father did. She wouldn't have mentioned it."

"Jodie was a *princess?*"

"As you will be, Suzanne, an hour from now, when you marry me. Technically, anyway," he added casually.

"That's—! That's—!" She pressed her hands to her hot cheeks. She'd intended to check her library for information about Aragovia, but there had been no time. To be honest, too, Stephen's origins had seemed unimportant in the face of her concern for Alice's future. Now, she regretted that she hadn't been more thorough, and that she hadn't questioned Dr. Feldman more closely. His words to her had contained some clues, but she'd ignored them.

Stephen smiled. It was a teasing, upside-down kind of expression that made the fine, tanned skin around his eyes crinkle and flattened the little dent near the corner of his top lip. "Don't get excited about it," he said, as if she were a child overreacting to the sight of a birthday cake.

"Excited?" she almost shrieked. "I'm not excited!" Although her mind was racing along like a river about to flood its banks. "I'm— It's impossible!"

"It's not," he said. He was like a small island of calm, with the wild waters of her mood swirling around him. "My great-grandfather was Prince Peter Christian Serkin-Rimsky of Aragovia. He married an Englishwoman, Lady Elizabeth Shrevebury in 1912, and commissioned these pieces as a wedding gift for her. My great-grandfather and his advisers were in the process of drafting a democratic constitution, when Communism took over. Our lands and our ancestral home were taken over by the State. Only a few of our possessions were saved and taken out of the country. These jewels were among those possessions. It's a long story, which I'll tell you another time."

"I can't wait!" she said, in a voice that crawled with sarcasm. "Dr. Feldman told me that he 'discounted the Aragovian thing.' I didn't understand what he meant. But he meant this, didn't he? Not just that Jodie and her father had their origins in some little country in Europe, but that they were tied to the place by royal heritage and royal blood."

"Yes." The single syllable was carefully spoken, after a pause. "This is what he meant."

"Was he right?" she demanded. "Should I 'discount the Aragovian thing?' Is it important? How much does your heritage matter in your life? You're

planning to sell these jewels to build a hospital. I'm
not sure what that suggests.''

"To turn most of the existing royal palace into a
hospital, but it amounts to the same thing, as it needs
extensive work,'' he agreed.

He hadn't quite answered her question, she noticed.

''Dr. Feldman said he thought you'd end up staying
here,'' she said. ''Is there a chance of that? After all,
you're not a prince anymore, in any real sense. They
can name the hospital after your family, and you can
leave. Make a future here, like your uncle did. The
place is, what, a democracy, now?''

He hesitated. Again. ''It is becoming one. Slowly.
There's a cultural legacy from the Communist years
to shake off, first.''

''So you could leave. You would, if that was best
for Alice. You said you'd live wherever was best for
Alice.'' They weren't questions anymore. They were
demands, and all she needed was his confirmation.

''My goal is to do what's best for Alice, yes,'' was
his cautious answer. All his replies had been cautious,
against her emotional questioning.

This answer caught her attention and slowed her
down. ''You're saying that as if you don't know yet
what best is.''

''That's reasonable, isn't it? Situations change. The
question of custody has to be decided first. The most
important thing is that she should grow up knowing
stability and love.''

''You sound like Michael.''

''He's right. Isn't that why we're getting married?
And we have a wedding ceremony to take part in.
Isn't that the first and most vital step?''

She could only nod. If they didn't go through with this… But she wished desperately that she had more time—time to think things through. She'd been so single-minded lately. Tunnel-visioned. She sensed that there were issues lurking in the corners of her mind, more questions she should be throwing at him, deeper connections she hadn't yet had a chance to make.

And, definitely, things he wasn't telling her.

The question she actually asked him was by no means the most important. "You want me to wear the tiara and the necklace today. Why?"

"I told you, didn't I? You will be the last Serkin-Rimsky bride to wear the only significant item left of my family's heritage."

"Then, yes, of course I'll wear them." That wasn't difficult. It didn't commit her to anything. It didn't endanger Alice in any way.

And perhaps it said something about the man who stood so close to her. Respect for tradition was a positive quality. Coupled with her memory of the way he'd so carefully put Alice's bootie away to send home to his mother—who was knitting, now!—it added up to something in him that she couldn't dismiss, something she was intrigued by, and drawn to.

She didn't know how to label it, but seized on it anyway. *Honor.* Was that the word? It was an old-fashioned one, but she'd always had a lot of respect for old-fashioned things.

She finished in a distracted way, "Of course I'll wear them. They're the most beautiful things I've ever seen."

There was a creak and the door to the street

opened, letting in the afternoon light. Rose entered, with Perry strolling languidly, close behind her. He was a handsome man in his late fifties, with a slim, well-proportioned build, a smooth face and attractively graying hair.

"Oh, you *are* here." Rose said, sounding a little breathless. "I called you at your apartment, but there was no answer. Darling, the bride isn't supposed to be early for her own wedding! She's supposed to keep everyone on tenterhooks, including the groom."

"Stephen and I had…something to talk about," Suzanne told her mother.

Instinctively, she had moved a little closer to him, and she could feel the warmth of his body radiating against her bare arm. She was still in a daze, and her mind buzzed louder than ever, but she had sense enough to realize that she had to present a united front to her mother, with the man she was about to marry.

Stephen had replaced the tiara in its box, and put both boxes in the carrier bag. Rose didn't notice the boxes, or the necklace that nestled against her skin. "Put on the other in front of the mirror," he said to Suzanne quietly, so that Rose and Perry did not hear.

"Mom, Perry, this is Stephen Serkin…uh…Serkin-Rimsky."

"Just Serkin will do today," he said.

"Stephen, this is my mother and stepfather. Rose and Perry Wigan."

"Your uncle always went by Rimsky," Rose commented. "It's nice to meet you."

She stretched out her hand and murmured something else that Suzanne didn't catch. Rose's look said it all, however. She was assessing Stephen as if he was the centerpiece platter on a buffet table, and evidently she was appreciative of what she saw. Rose had always liked a good-looking man, but said herself, frequently, that it had never done her any good.

Still dressed in his faded jeans, plain T-shirt and fraying athletic shoes, Stephen looked like an ordinary, good-looking American male, who didn't care a whole lot about what he wore as long as it was clean and comfortable. He obviously didn't want to announce his royal lineage through his appearance, but no clothing could have diminished the healthy glow of his masculinity.

The soft hug of the T-shirt hinted at the strong, smooth muscles beneath. The worn side seams of the jeans emphasized the lean length of his thighs. No man had the right to look that good in such ancient, casual clothing. Perry's elaborate pale gray suit and satin waistcoat looked pompous and two-dimensional in comparison, and Perry was his usual indolent, half-asleep self.

"Darling, I've brought you something, if it's not too late for you to fix it in place," Rose said, turning her hundred-watt gaze away from Stephen and onto her daughter. "My wedding veil, for good luck. You should be very thankful, because Perry and I had to drive all the way down to Philly and back to bring it, and it took an hour of rummaging in the attic before I could find it. Perry had me on a clock, didn't you, darling?" She smirked at her husband, who smirked back.

"Your veil! Oh, Mom, thanks!"

Suzanne's eyes misted as Rose took the froth of tulle from a plain calico storage bag and heaped it into her arms. She hadn't even realized that Rose had kept it.

Rose's marriage to Suzanne's father had taken place more than twenty-eight years ago. It hadn't been a success, and it had finally failed just two months after Jill's birth. They hadn't seen their father in more than twenty years, and had no idea where he was, or if he was even still alive.

But the veil meant something, all the same. Maybe Mom was right in what she had said on Wednesday at her hotel. This whole thing needn't become a battle, if Rose would only see that loving Alice came first, and that Suzanne was the one who could do that most faithfully.

"You'll have to use hairpins to fasten it," Rose was saying briskly. "I brought some with me."

"So did I, to put my hair up."

"We'll do it together, shall we, darling? A bride should have her mother's help when she gets dressed."

Her voice fogged thickly, and Suzanne was touched despite the difficulties between them.

She didn't feel so sentimental a few minutes later, after she'd taken the tiara from its box and placed it on her head.

"This will keep the veil in place," she told Rose almost shyly.

Having had a little time to adjust to Stephen's revelation, she could appreciate the significance of the heavy circlet she held in her hands. It was a gift of love from a prince to his bride. That was more precious, more magical, than its monetary value. Was it possible that some of the magic could rub off, could lay a luster of hope over this practical, necessary ceremony, and the marriage that would follow?

"Isn't it beautiful?" she continued. "It matches the necklace."

She scraped her hair back from her neck so that Rose could see it better, but Rose made no comment beyond a little hiss of shock.

"I'll put my hair up," Suzanne said instead, and found the barrettes and pins she'd brought to fix it in place, high on her head. A twist or two, a few intricate movements with her fingers, and it was done. Not nearly as good as an expensive salon styling, but neat and soft and ready for Rose's veil.

"Hmm...so where did you get those gaudy things, then?" Rose questioned at last, her eye on the necklace and tiara and her voice overly casual.

"They belong to Stephen's family. I don't think they're gaudy." She traced the curved edges of gold on the necklace at her throat with one finger. "Not at all."

"Well, no," Rose conceded. "They'd be gorgeous, if they were real."

"They are real, Mom."

At this, Rose burst into laughter. "What? Alex Rimsky's nephew has jewelry like that? Alex was penniless when he came to the U.S.!"

"They're heirlooms. He keeps them in a bank vault, here in New York." Why here? Suzanne wondered briefly. Stephen himself had said it was a long story. She could only explain to Rose the little of it that she knew. "They were made for his great-grandmother, Princess Elizabeth of Aragovia, in 1912."

"You're joking, right? *Princess* Elizabeth?"

"No, I'm not joking. He told me all about it."

"So I suppose that makes your Stephen a prince? And Alex, for that matter."

"Yes," Suzanne answered. She lifted her chin, then added the same word Stephen himself had chosen. "Technically."

"Honey, don't you think Alex would have told me?"

"Apparently he'd turned his back on all that when he decided to make his future here. Royalty wasn't exactly popular in the Soviet Union, and it wasn't relevant in the United States. The two of you didn't know each other very long, did you? No, I don't think Alex would have told you at all. I've talked to Dr. Feldman about some of this, though, and it's true."

"Okay, so technically you're going to become a princess in a few minutes! Let's accept that at face value," Rose said in a sugary, inviting tone. Then the sugar shattered. "Guess what? It doesn't mean squat, honey! Princes can be con men just like anyone else."

"Stephen's not," Suzanne answered, very sure of herself on that point.

"In case you've forgotten," Rose added, "Alice is a very rich little baby, and I'm sure Alex Rimsky's nephew knows that. He wants to get his hands on her money, and he's conning you, with that pretty jewelry of his, into thinking money's not important to him because he's a *prince*. If there ever were any originals to model those pieces on, they were sold or stolen long ago."

"I don't believe that."

"Believe it! This is called a bait-and-switch scam,

honey, and you'd better keep your eyes well and truly open.''

''I don't believe you,'' Suzanne said again.

There was a short silence, then Rose said lightly, ''No, of course you don't. Daughters never believe home truths from their mothers. But Feldman will.''

She paused, and Suzanne could see the wheels turning in her head. Rose Wigan wasn't a clever woman, but she was devious. She felt a shiver run down her spine, beneath the cool satin of her dress.

''Especially when he finds out that you're not even living together,'' Rose went on.

''We will be. We'll share the apartment. We haven't had time to plan—''

''No, I bet you haven't. This marriage is going to be a more obvious fake than that tiara.''

''I—we—''

Suzanne could barely breathe. The implied threat behind Rose's words was like a fist slammed into her gut, though Rose's tone hadn't lost its cooing sweetness.

''Thought not. Honey, shall I tell him, or will you?'' Rose's hand brushed a light caress on Suzanne's arm.

''Tell who? Tell him what?''

''Tell your froggy prince that the wedding is off, of course.''

''But it isn't off. It's happening, Mom.''

Anger had begun to build inside her, but she held it there, didn't let it escape, instinctively sensing that it gave her more power that way.

Rose, at this moment, didn't have the same control.

''Darling, what's the point?'' The cooing voice

cracked, and her teeth were clenched. "You know you can't win Alice this way. I'm going to talk to Feldman as soon as I can."

"So talk to him! Do it, Mom!"

In her mind's eye, Suzanne could see Alice, felt like she could almost touch her. It was the same picture she had carried inside her heart since last week, when she and Stephen had stood together beside the baby's transparent Plexiglas crib and watched her smiling in her sleep. It gave her a strength and determination she'd never known before, even though she'd come through with both those qualities more than once in her life already.

"Talk to him!" she repeated, icily calm.

"Suzanne, admit defeat now!" Rose snarled in frustration, glaring at the dress and the necklace and the tiara as if she loathed every thread and every link of precious metal. "The marriage isn't going to be real, whether you're sharing an apartment or not."

"No?" Suzanne retorted. "No, Mom? *Then prove it!*"

Suzanne was white.

Stephen saw it at once, and was shocked at the difference it made to her face, beneath the dark pile of her hair and the glittering crescent of the tiara. It was as if the color had bled from her cheeks into the slash of deep matte pink which she'd applied to her lips.

Her pallor wasn't the only thing that shocked him. Her eyes glittered and her fists were clenched. Brides shouldn't walk down the aisle with clenched fists.

He was waiting at the altar, dressed in the plain,

dark suit he'd bought a few days ago, and Father Davenport, in his ministering robes, stood waiting, also. There was no music. Suzanne had her hand on Perry Wigan's arm. She looked as if she would rather have been clutching a live snake. Rose had appointed herself matron of honor and was leading the way, her smile fixed and brittle.

What had happened between the two of them, down in that back room where Suzanne had dressed?

They had been absent for a while. Stephen had plenty of time to find the men's bathroom, put on his suit and bundle his street clothes into a bag. He'd returned to the church and taken up his position at the front, expecting only a short wait.

Perry had made an awkward companion, sitting in the front pew. Both of them were wary of each other. Neither of them wanted to talk. Stephen was as unimpressed with Perry's snakelike qualities as Suzanne now appeared to be.

But her dislike of the man wasn't at the root of the tension in her, Stephen could tell. She looked like a block of marble, and when she reached him her eyes swam and flamed and stormed with silent, desperate messages that he didn't understand.

Instinctively, he took her hands, and Father Davenport took this as his signal to begin the ceremony. Stephen hardly heard the preamble to the vows. Suzanne's fingers were ice-cold. He rubbed his thumbs back and forth over them, tried to engulf them in his warm palms, but could make little impression on their temperature.

With eyes still fixed on him, she spoke. He didn't understand. Something about Alice? "Alice to be real.'' It didn't make sense, but he nodded automatically, all the same, and made a soothing, meaningless sound. Anything to get that desperate, terrified, suffering look off her face!

It seemed to work, a little. She relaxed enough to allow both of them to pick up their cues from Father Davenport and get through their vows without stumbling. They were powerful words, a reminder that the institution of marriage was bigger than any two individuals who entered it.

Once again, Stephen thought of his great-grandmother, the first and last woman, until now, to wear these glittering jewels as a bride. She had loved Prince Peter enough to leave her life in England behind, and to remain with him through all the torments of the Soviet regime, through war and poverty, grief and loss. Their marriage had lasted for sixty-eight years, ending with Peter's death in 1980. Elizabeth had lived on as a widow for another nine years.

The bride who stood in front of him today had very different needs to those of Great-grandmother Elizabeth, a different heritage, different priorities, different strengths, but he thought he understood them. A dozen hopes and regrets tangled inside him, and the future seemed impossibly unknowable.

Then suddenly, it was over. They were man and wife. Father Davenport gave one last instruction that Stephen missed. What was he supposed to do? In the emotion of the moment, he'd forgotten anything he ever knew about American wedding customs. He saw Suzanne swaying forward, and felt her hands clutching the stiff sleeves of his suit.

Her mouth was just inches from his, and her eyes

were fixed on his face, wide and pleading. He only just managed to catch her words, they were spoken so low.

"Kiss me," she said. *"Please kiss me!"*

Then, without waiting for him to respond, she cupped his jaw in her palms and crushed her mouth passionately against his.

Chapter Four

Stephen felt the fire of desperation in the way Suzanne kissed, and wondered if she'd ever kissed a man this way before in her life. It was bold and sensuous and demanding.

Even if he'd wanted to, it would have taken an effort for him to pull away. And he didn't want to. Only a fraction of a second passed before he began to return the kiss in full, parting her lips with his. He wrapped his arms around her, and his pulses leaped at the feel of satin and skin at the open neckline of her dress.

He could hardly tell where the dress left off and she began. Both textures were warm and smooth, giving beneath his touch. But most giving of all was her mouth. It was warm, full, sure and tasted faintly of strawberries.

Now that he had responded, her boldness had gone, replaced by a compliant, melting softness that told him she was as moved—as overwhelmed—by this as he was. Her fingers stroked his jawline then sank to his shoulders, gripping him there as if she might fall without his support.

He was pleased that both her motivation and her response were so strong, found himself hoping that she never had kissed a man this way, never come close in her life.

Save kisses like this for me, Suzanne.

He was then immediately appalled by his own arrogance. Appalled, yes, but that didn't stop him from wanting to test his power. He was prepared to be ruthless, for the sake of Alice's destiny.

Deliberately, he deepened the kiss, slid his hands down her back and felt her response intensify. A shiver of need rippled through her and her breasts pressed against his chest. She wasn't pretending. For both of them, this was very real.

"Suzanne," he murmured, and loved the sweet taste of her name on his tongue. "Suzanne…"

"Yes," she said. "Yes…"

She must have interpreted his words as a plea to end their kiss, because her mouth drifted away from his at last and she turned to face her mother. One hand slid down his shoulder and she gripped the sleeve of his suit, crumpling the fine, new wool.

"Congratulations!" Rose said. Her eyes glittered as they darted back and forth between Stephen and Suzanne. Her mouth was pursed, and she looked shocked.

Even Father Davenport seemed a little surprised at the length and heat of their kiss. He recovered quickly, however, and confined Suzanne in a brief hug.

"I hope you'll be very happy, my dear," he said. "David always predicted you'd do well in life."

Rose hardly permitted her daughter to hear the quiet compliment, let alone respond to it.

"Darling," she said, "A mother needs to kiss her girl. This is the happiest day of my life!"

Her voice shook as she hugged and kissed Suzanne. Stephen noted the fact, filed it away. He kept an open mind about it, at this stage.

Either she cares, or it's a good performance, he decided. Whichever the case, he didn't want to underestimate Rose as a player in this game. He could see how his uncle would have been attracted to her, so many years ago. She must have been a beautiful and vivacious girl, possessing a wild streak that a virile twenty-nine-year-old immigrant, with the heat of ambition and adventure in his blood, would have found hard to resist.

And she was still beautiful and graceful, in a close-fitting ivory silk suit, defying the convention that no one but the bride should wear bridal colors.

"And Stephen, my new son-in-law!" Rose turned to him now, then added, over her shoulder, "Perry, honey, can you imagine that I'm old enough to have a married daughter?"

"Hardly!" Perry replied with a sleepy smile.

With Stephen, Rose's hug was a mere sketch of movement, stiff and automatic and over in a moment. Then she held him at arm's length and looked into his eyes.

"Look after her," she said. Tears still brimmed at

her mascara-stiffened lashes. "She's so precious to me. Love at first sight is a magical thing...."

What?

"...but now the hard work begins. If you hurt her, you'll answer to me for it. A rushed marriage like yours could be in the hands of divorce lawyers within weeks. I'd hate to see that."

Ah, okay. Stephen understood her change of strategy now.

"I think Suzanne and I are both mature enough to know what we want," he answered, his voice steady and cool and deliberate. "It's not love at first sight. It's something else, with much more enduring importance."

"We'll see," Rose said. Her smile stopped halfway up her face. "We'll see, won't we?"

They both knew it was a threat, and so did Suzanne. Stephen felt the crook of her arm lock into place around his elbow. Her lips looked pale and dry, although they hadn't been a few moments ago when he'd kissed them.

"I don't suppose there's a honeymoon planned, is there?" Perry roused himself to ask. "After a wedding arranged at such short notice?"

He had moved to stand beside Rose, who shot him an appreciative glance. John Davenport was looking back and forth between the two couples with a frown on his face, sensing that there was much more to all this than showed on the surface.

At Perry's question, Stephen felt Suzanne stiffen. He dropped his arm across her shoulders to pull her more tightly against him, and cut off her answer before she could open her mouth.

"There's very definitely a honeymoon," he said. "We have the use of a friend's apartment overlooking Central Park, for the next week."

"Stephen?" Suzanne said, turning to him with widened eyes.

"You'd better run that detail past your bride one more time," Rose said with a satisfied smile. "She doesn't seem to know anything about it."

Stephen produced a polite laugh. "Well, hardly, since it's a surprise—part of my wedding gift to her. I've ordered a limousine, Suzanne, to take us to your apartment and wait while you pack, before driving us to Fifth Avenue. That will save time, because I know you'll want to fit in a visit to Alice today as well."

"Don't worry about Alice," Rose said. "She'll have her Grandma to keep her company. Do you know, John, that darling baby actually *smiled* for me yesterday, for the very first time in her life?"

She put a warm, confiding hand on Father Davenport's forearm and began to talk to him about Alice, interrupting herself finally to say, "Stephen, Suzanne. I think I hear your limo out front. Honey, we'll be meeting at the hospital every day, I should think, so I won't make a big deal about saying goodbye to my newly married girl."

"That's fine, Mom, no one needs to make a big deal out of anything," Suzanne said, and felt Stephen's hand slide against hers.

"Your mother is right," he said. "It's our car out front. Let's go, shall we?"

"See you at the hospital, honey," Rose said.

"Yes."

"I'm afraid we forgot to bring any rice or confetti," Perry drawled.

"I won't hold it against you," Suzanne told him. She ducked a kiss from her stepfather by hurrying after Stephen, down the aisle.

Stephen smiled at her as soon as they reached the bright afternoon light outside.

"There," he said. "That part's done. And we achieved the right effect, I think."

"Yes." The word *effect* sent a little chill through her, but she couldn't deny that it was appropriate. This marriage was very definitely designed with certain effects in view. "Thank you for thinking so quickly about the honeymoon. I'd have agreed with Perry that we had nothing planned, and that wouldn't have sounded good. Knowing Mom, she'll call my apartment to check if I'm there, so I'd better not pick up for the next week."

"You won't be there to pick up. You'll be honeymooning with me on Fifth Avenue."

She stopped in her tracks, halfway down the church steps. "I thought you were just saying that."

"We can't afford to lie, Suzanne," he said. He smiled at her, his thin silver scar and his two crooked teeth the only imperfections in the commanding impression he made. "What's at stake is too important. Yes, I arranged a honeymoon. It's a seven-room apartment. Three bedrooms. No one needs to know how many of them we actually use."

Suzanne's suitcase mocked her attempts at clear thinking. It sat on the double bed in the undivided loft apartment, open and still half-empty, although not as empty as the apartment itself.

Suzanne could see Stephen assessing the uninterrupted expanse of hardwood flooring, and the series of heavy black floor-to-ceiling drapes, each pulled to one side. He looked skeptical, which wasn't a surprise. The place had once served as a theater company's rehearsal space, and hadn't changed much since. There was a television, a double bed, dresser, a couch and a microwave, and that was about all. The bathroom was the only separate space. Even the kitchen was just a line of appliances and a section of countertop along the south wall, beside the door.

Stephen switched on the television, as if seeking a distraction, and it filled the echoing space with metallic sound. In the street below, the elegant white limousine with its tinted windows was waiting for them. It was an incongruous sight this far toward the river in the area known as Hell's Kitchen on New York's midtown west side.

Suzanne had been lucky to get this four-month rental so cheaply, from a minor Broadway actor away on an out-of-town tour. This, she hoped, was the home she would bring Alice to, within the next week. Beyond that, she hadn't thought about where the two of them—the three of them?—would live permanently. She knew only that all of her decisions on the future would be guided by Alice's well-being, and couldn't succeed in bringing Stephen into the picture in her mind.

Even the rest of today seemed like a blank slate to her.

"I don't know what to pack," she told Stephen

helplessly, over the sound of an old sitcom's canned laugh track. "This isn't making sense, right now. That we've just gotten married, and you're here in this apartment."

"Apartment? It's a warehouse!" he said.

"I like it."

"For a tiny baby?"

He had a point.

"We'll work something out," she said defensively. "It has good heating. It's temporary, and I could afford it. I didn't have time to shop around."

Although she was fighting him, she felt diminished by his implied criticism, reminded of how Mom always made her feel. Where Mom would have sensed her advantage and circled to attack—very sweetly— from another quarter, however, Stephen apologized.

"I'm being unfair," he said. "Of course you didn't. And you're right. I've lived in worse circumstances. We can make something of this, for as long as we have to."

"We..." Don't go there. It's too hard. Stick with today. Stick with now. "Yes. I'll pack," she said, finding the beginnings of her own strength again.

"And tomorrow we'll go shopping together, for Alice's homecoming," he promised. "We'll make it work."

By the time the rented car nosed its way into the northward stream of traffic along Tenth Avenue, it was peak hour, and their journey uptown and across to Fifth Avenue took time.

"We may have to wait until tonight to see the baby," Stephen said.

"I was going to suggest that we wait anyway," she

answered him. "I'm not going to turn this into a competition."

"It is a competition, isn't it? A fight for a child's heart."

"You heard Mom talking to John at the church," she answered him. "Mom was stealing my stories about Alice's smile, and about how I felt when she came off the respirator, as if they were hers. She wasn't even there! But you can bet she's going to be there from now on! She'll cancel her plan to go back to Philly on Monday and stay until after the custody hearing."

"Yes, I got that impression, too."

"But I'm not going to turn it into a marathon, see who can last the distance, who can impress Feldman and the nurses the most. That's not why I've spent all these weeks beside her little crib."

"I know it's not, Suzanne."

"I wasn't trying to impress anyone. I was there to make her stay alive. Just to *force* her, with the strength of my love, my voice and my touch, to stay alive. I won't betray her, or myself, by making it into a marathon!" she repeated.

Her voice was husky and she felt a tear splash onto the bare skin just below her collarbone. He saw it, reached out a forefinger and brushed it away before it rolled down to stain the fragile satin of her dress. It was the tiniest touch, but they both froze. Her gaze locked with his and then he brought his hand slowly back to his thigh.

Over. The tear was gone. His finger was gone. Safe.

She began to breathe again. Actually, why had she stopped breathing in the first place?

Oh. Okay. This was why. This. It wasn't over at all....

His mouth moved sweet and slow on hers, as if he were afraid, at first, that he might frighten her off. His hands were gentle, asking questions not issuing commands. Oh, but she wasn't scared at all, even though she probably should have been.

The car's long leather seat was too wide. They both had to lean in order to reach. Closing her eyes to blindly savor the heat of his mouth, she felt the satin neckline slip a little, felt his caress tracing the slopes of newly exposed skin. Again, just a finger, a single, soft, teasing finger, whispering its seductive secrets across her breasts in a language without words.

She didn't need language. She knew what this meant. His hands slid across her hips, cupping her bottom through the flared skirts of the dress and pulling her closer. She went willingly, stunned by the power of her response to him. Had to cling to him— to the lapels of his suit jacket, to the fine Sea Island cotton of his shirt, to the warm skin at his waist, just to keep from drowning. That was how it felt. That Stephen...his mouth...his body...was the only solid reality in the universe at this moment.

The limousine crawled across town at Fifty-Seventh Street. Stopped at a succession of red lights, it was surrounded by commuters leaving work and heading for the subway. They surged around the car in harried, hurrying waves, the noise of their feet, of vehicle engines, of trains running beneath the street, and even of the blaring horns of cars and trucks muffled into a benign roar by the darkly tinted, soundproofed windows.

No one could see the two of them. No one knew that they were here, like this. Doing this. Feeling this. Stephen slid the gown from her shoulders and stroked each rounded knob of bone and muscle with his thumbs as his mouth teased her ear. She clung to his back, had to fight to keep from digging into his flesh with her nails. When his mouth trailed to the upper slopes of her breasts and his fingers—impatient, now—flicked her bra straps aside, she gasped.

"It's so good, to feel what I'm doing to you," he muttered. "To hear it in the way you breathe, to feel it through your fingers, to see it..."

Her nipples had hardened like two stones. He slipped his hand beneath satin and lace, and cupped one breast, his thumb tracing lazy circles around the achingly sensitive skin that surrounded the nubbed crest.

She watched, haunted by his focus. She couldn't see his eyes. They were hidden behind the sweep of his lashes. Then his head bent lower, he lifted the weight of her breast free of the final barrier of fabric and touched his lips softly to her nipple. She gave a moan, closed her eyes and sank against the cool leather, willing him to go on. This. More. Anything. Everything.

Don't stop.

She would have said it aloud, but his mouth had closed over hers once more and she couldn't speak. Hungrily, she wound her arms around his neck and tasted him deeply. Just couldn't let go. That life-raft feeling again. She *needed* this, the way she needed air and food and sunlight.

"We're almost there, Suzanne," he said. His voice

was burred, deeper than usual. "Heaven knows, I could go on with this—" He shook his head, pressed his lips together.

"I know."

She watched his face as he gently slid her bra straps up, cupped her breasts once more in his hands, then pulled the dress into place on her shoulders.

"I can't stop looking at you," he said.

"Then don't," she answered. Couldn't begin to hide her need. "I—like it, Stephen. Can't you tell?"

"Yes, sweetheart, I can tell. It's good."

A minute later, they had pulled up in front of the dark green awning of an elegant pale stone building just off Fifth Avenue, and the driver had the door open ready for Suzanne to step out. She straightened her twisted dress clumsily, feeling the evening air striking cold on her skin after the warmth of Stephen's body heat against her.

The doorman took her suitcase. Stephen had brought his things here earlier, apparently. He'd had the key to this apartment for several days. The lobby was a symphony of marble and gold, and the elevator was elegant and slow. On the seventh floor, Suzanne glimpsed a huge vase of fresh flowers set in an alcove. She stood beside Stephen in front of a dark, panelled door, heard the click and rattle of his key in the lock.

The door swung open, and she began to move forward, but he put down the suitcase he'd taken from the doorman in the lobby and held her back.

"There's a tradition at this point, I think," he said.

"Oh. Yes. But, um—"

"I think it would be unwise of us to ignore it, Suzanne."

"Would it?"

His answer was just to scoop her up in his arms and bundle her across the threshold, his gaze holding her prisoner, his smile daring her to protest and his breath warm on her neck.

"You can put me down, now," she said breathlessly.

"I'm tempted not to. I wonder how long I could carry you like this?"

"Put...me...down.... And stop making me smile!"

He did as she'd asked, setting her so lightly on the floor that she felt like a ballerina. "Better now?"

"Much better!"

Until she actually took a breath and looked at the place, that is. It was gorgeous. Original oil paintings, acres of immaculate carpet, framed mirrors. Side tables, coffee tables, armoires and escritoires, ornaments of ivory and crystal and jade.

Suddenly, it jarred. *Everything* jarred.

She turned to Stephen, felt goose bumps rising on her chilled skin and said, "I don't understand. Tell me about this place. Who does it belong to? If you've had the key for days, why were you staying at a cheap hotel that's for tourists? And why did you walk around my ugly, unfinished warehouse of an apartment talking about making it work, as if you'd even *consider* living there, after a place like this. It doesn't make sense. *You* don't make sense, Prince Stephen of Aragovia."

"No, I suppose I don't," he agreed. He leaned over the back of a pale lemon-colored couch, his fingers splayed against the jacquard weave of the fabric. "It takes some getting used to, you see. I'm not entirely comfortable in these elegant surroundings.''

"Yeah, tell me about it!'' she agreed. She'd never been in a place like this in her life.

"My family has lived and struggled like anyone else,'' he continued. "But things have started to change, now that I am free to use my title without fear of harm.''

"Harm? To *you?*''

He ran a finger down the scar on his face. "Twice, in the past ten years, assassins in the pay of the Russian mafia have been hired to kill me. Once, as you can see, they came close.''

"Why?"

"Because of the threat I represented,'' he said. "My family had always been popular. There were always those who hoped a Serkin-Rimsky prince or princess would rule in Aragovia again. The possibility of my family acting as a rallying point for all those who hated the Russian-controlled gangs made me a danger to their power base. If the two rival groups hadn't destroyed each other when they did, I would have had to leave the country. I was becoming too much of a danger to the people I cared about. My mother was beside herself with worry....''

"You still haven't explained all this.'' The sweep of her arm took in the space, the furnishings, the park views on two sides.

"My uncle Alex wasn't the only Aragovian immigrant who made a success of his life in the United States, Suzanne. This apartment belongs to another Aragovian nobleman who became a refugee from the devastation of Central Europe in 1945. Arkady Radouleau is now a very successful dealer in fine arts, and he would like to see my family's name restored. He and his wife, Sonia, are on a buying trip to Europe at the moment, so the apartment was free, but I didn't feel comfortable about using it until I had a good reason to.''

"Our honeymoon, for Mom's benefit."

"You'll have to get used to this—to the fact that there are people whom you've never met who want to help. People you've never met that are happy and hopeful about our marriage."

She nodded silently. Might have asked some more questions if his next words hadn't distracted her.

"And I've had to tell myself the same thing," he said. "I'm not a struggling student, as I was when Jodie and I became friends."

"You'll be living like a struggling student at my apartment!"

"It's a lifestyle, believe me, to which I've had plenty of opportunity to accustom myself."

"You're very adaptable." Even as she said it, she didn't know if it was a compliment or a challenge.

"I have to be. I've trained myself to be. It's not hard, when you have a guiding light in view."

"Tell me about your guiding light. I'm not sure that I know what it is. Alice, of course, or—?"

But he hadn't heard. Or, at any rate, he didn't reply. He'd picked up her suitcase to take to the main bedroom. Her bedroom, apparently.

Theirs? came the sudden thought, so graphic that it was like a photograph in her mind. Click! She could see the bedroom through the open door, and it was huge. What color were the sheets, beneath that puffy blue-and-white comforter? The same shade of powder blue, edged with white cotton lace?

She could see herself…feel herself…waking beside him in that bed in the morning, warm and sleepy, sated and content. They were married, weren't they?

Yes, but they were married for a reason. A *different* reason.

So what about the way you felt in the limo?

She shivered again, found the heating control and turned it up. Even a place as luxurious as this could get damp and chilly when it wasn't used. Following Stephen into the master bedroom, she saw the awareness in his eyes as he glanced between her and the bed.

"I'll take one of the other bedrooms," he said.

They both knew that wouldn't last long. Suzanne didn't dare to think about what it meant. Her mother had talked about "love at first sight" today. Rose had meant it maliciously, as a taunt, a castle in the air that she'd take pleasure, later on, in knocking to the ground, but… How fast could love grow? This pull, this need, was that what love meant?

No, love at first sight—love, when you'd known a man for less than two weeks—was for fairy tales.

Yes, and princes were for fairy tales, too.

She didn't need a prince in her life. She didn't need love at first or second sight. All she needed was a father for Alice. She was beginning to suspect, however, that in Stephen she'd taken on a whole lot more than that.

Chapter Five

"Shall we find somewhere quiet to eat?" Stephen asked.

"Yes, I'd like that."

"And then we'll see Alice."

"I'm glad you're planning to come."

"Of course I am."

Suzanne had changed into jeans and a thin pink cotton sweater, knitted in a classic Aran pattern. No more heeled satin slippers on her feet, but a pair of flat, slip-on shoes in a pink that matched her sweater. The priceless Aragovian jewelry was safely stored in this luxury apartment's hidden wall safe. It would be returned to the bank vault on Monday.

If Suzanne was sending a message with the casual clothing, then Stephen had received it loud and clear. He didn't want to fight it, either.

He'd kissed her very deliberately in the privacy of the limousine, but he hadn't intended it to go as far as it had. Definitely hadn't planned for the painful rush of blood to his groin the moment she'd come into the master bedroom a few minutes ago. Since when had the combination of two fully clothed people and a large bed possessed so much erotic power?

Their attraction to each other meshed with his needs and his plans, but he must not let it go too far. He must keep it within his own control. He knew what came first in his life. Aragovia. Alice and her destiny. The unspoiled heart of a people who still had faith in his family's royal name even after more than eighty years of living as ordinary citizens.

No woman could take precedence over all that.

Would he sleep with Suzanne tonight, then? He was married to her. It was an obvious expectation, and one which he'd talked about with her, if very briefly. But he sensed her essential innocence. If she wasn't a virgin physically, then he suspected she was virginal where it counted even more—in her heart. No man had truly touched her core. No man had made her sob his name with a mix of love and desire strong enough to fill her whole world.

This knowledge chafed uneasily against Stephen's sense of honor. It would be so very easy to sleep with her. Tonight, tomorrow, next week. He could see, in his mind, the way she would move with her legs wrapped around him. He could smell her musky female scent, and hear her moans. She had moaned in the limousine, just a tiny, fluttery sound in her throat, and it had sent sharp darts of longing through him. He knew he could make her moan with ten times as much intensity as that.

But would it be right?

Shrugging his shoulders into his old leather bomber jacket—the one he hung on to, and loved, because it reminded him of a simpler time, when his responsibilities had seemed far less—he was startled to discover that his hands were shaking with the effort of pushing down his erotic thoughts of her.

He grabbed the keys he'd tossed into a glass dish on the rosewood hall table, checked that he had transferred his wallet from wedding suit to casual pants and growled, "Let's go, then, shall we?"

"Oh, I should get my jacket, too."

Don't, he wanted to say. *Because then I'll lose those tiny glimpses of what has to be your wedding bra—those lovely shapes of pale satin and lace—beneath your sweater.*

Instead, he just nodded, and as soon as she'd left in search of her jacket he swore in Russian. He added another very colorful oath in Aragovian—the language, related to Romanian, which the Soviet system hadn't been able to stamp out in his people after more than half a century of trying. For good measure, he finished with a triple rendition of the word "Damn!" in English, and felt sufficiently distracted from his torment to actually leave the apartment at her side.

They took the subway down to Twenty-Third Street and had steak, salad and fries in the back of a quiet diner. Neither of them wanted to talk much, but their frequent silences seemed nourishing and easy, rather than awkward.

With time to watch her across the softly lit table, nothing getting in the way, Stephen could see that Suzanne's fatigue ran bone deep. It was the emotional and physical exhaustion that came from keeping her lengthy daily vigils at the hospital, of never sleeping long enough or soundly enough, of being chased and haunted day and night by dark questions not only about Alice's future, but about her very life.

And Suzanne had handled all of it on her own. The emotional support of her sisters and the occasional piece of practical assistance from Michael Feldman couldn't count for much. Stephen wondered how on earth she juggled the irregular hours of her library job, not to mention little things like eating and laundry and paying bills. It was hardly surprising that her apartment seemed as much like her home as a bus station waiting room.

Most people would have collapsed under the strain weeks ago. She was obviously a lot stronger than she looked, as he'd suspected from the beginning. Strong because of her single-minded love for Alice, strong in her determination to do whatever it took to keep the baby she loved. But no one could keep going like that forever.

I must look after her. The thought was instinctive. *I must cherish her. If she'll let me.*

"You're frowning," she said.

"So are you."

"Oh!" She laughed, her mouth curved upside down. Then she lifted her fingers to her forehead, smoothing the fine skin. "I guess I am. I think I've forgotten how to stop."

"Maybe you won't have so much to frown about in future," he suggested softly.

But when they reached Manhattan's Chelsea West-side Hospital, they found Rose snoozing in a chair beside Alice's crib, and Suzanne's frown was immediately back in place, deeper and darker than ever.

"I thought she'd have gone by now," she murmured.

"Does it matter?"

"I'm not a good actress, Stephen."

"You don't have to be, do you? What you feel is genuine."

"I lose touch with what I feel when Mom's around."

He didn't understand at first, not until he saw it for himself.

At the sound of their approach, Rose awoke, stretched, yawned and smiled, as sensuous as a well-fed lioness.

"Heavens, is that the time?" she said. There was a clock on a nearby wall, reading eight-fifteen.

"Have you been here long, Mom?"

"I came straight from the church, honey. Hello, Stephen. I hope you're looking after my little girl. Suzanne will tell you I've never yet let a man treat my daughter wrong, have I honey? You remember? And I don't plan on starting now."

Somehow, the words contained a threat, and it wasn't directed at Stephen.

"You should get something to eat, Mom." Suzanne's voice was stiff, thin.

"Oh, I can't leave her yet. Not when she's awake. She might smile at me again."

"She mostly smiles in her sleep, and she never stays awake more than about twenty minutes at a stretch."

"You will smile for your Gwanny, though, won't

you, boodyful? You'll stay awake for hours and hours, if your own speshul Gwanny plays wiv you.'' Rose cooed over the crib, making elaborate gestures and faces. "Nursey said you can have a wee snuggle in Gwanny's arms soon, gorgeoush.''

"Don't overstimulate her, Mom. It stresses her out.''

"Are you going to hold her tonight, Suzanne?'' Terri asked, as she checked the baby's heart and oxygen monitors.

"I don't think so. Not tonight.'' The brief reply was awkward. "We can't stay long. I like holding her when it's quiet.''

Stephen saw Terri's quick, surprised glance. She didn't say anything. Neither did Suzanne. But the more Rose cooed over the baby—it was a little over the top, sure, but many people got silly around babies—the stiffer and more distant Suzanne became. When she looked at Rose, her tight face smoked in resentment. Someone who'd never met her before would have quickly assumed that she wasn't interested in Alice, and that she didn't care.

A tall, balding man with a slight paunch and very long legs appeared at the far end of the unit and came toward them. Dr. Feldman, Stephen recognized.

"I had a patient in pediatric intensive care,'' he said. The bright lights of the unit reflected off his glasses. "And thought I'd stop in here as well. Rose, it's good to see you. Suzanne, Stephen.''

"Three visitors at once,'' Terri interjected. "Special treat, because we're hoping she'll go home next week.''

Would Suzanne's apartment really be Alice's

home, or just a temporary way station? Nobody brought up the issue.

"I'm going to get to hold her tonight, Michael," Rose said. "Isn't that incredible? It's great to be learning all this stuff that I'm going to need, like about her breathing and all. Are you sure you don't want to hold her as well, Suzanne, honey?"

"It's such a process, with her feed tube and her monitors and everything," Suzanne answered, in the same unnatural tone that her normally sweet voice had become imprisoned in. "I'd hate to stress her. You know she's still having the episodes of apnea." Stephen noted her familiarity with the medical term. It meant "not breathing," and was the reason Alice was still on oxygen and an alarm.

"It was nice to see you, Dr. Feldman," Suzanne added. "We have to leave now, don't we, Stephen?"

"You two came here together?" Michael Feldman asked.

Rose gave a soft laugh.

"We—well, we met up, and—" Suzanne stammered.

At best it was an avoidance of the facts, and of course Rose didn't let her daughter get away with it. Seeing it coming, Stephen winced.

"Met up?" Rose mimicked. "These two crazy lovebirds went and got themselves married today, Michael! A highly contagious case of love at first sight, apparently, since they only *met up* last week."

"It wasn't like that," Suzanne said, her tone gruff with rebellion. "You know it wasn't, Mom. Don't do this to me again. I'm not going to let Dr. Feldman think— It's stupid to pretend."

"Suzanne, I had no idea!" The doctor turned to her, visibly uncertain as to how he should react. He stretched his neck back to look at her, as if he needed a stronger prescription for his glasses. "Congratulations," he added automatically.

Rose stepped in confidently to guide his response.

"Remember the old saying about marrying in haste and repenting at leisure?" she said. "It doesn't hold true these days, does it? Young people rush to the altar the moment there's a hint of chemistry, safe in the knowledge that a quick fix divorce can make the other person disappear in a puff of smoke, the moment the novelty wears off."

"You've been married three times, Mom," Suzanne interjected. "I guess you would be an authority."

Mistake. Stephen saw her bite her bottom lip. She wasn't arguing her case well. He would have to try to explain the situation frankly to Dr. Feldman later. That they'd married for Alice's sake, but had strong hopes for their future together. It was true as far as it went.

"And I've been divorced once," Rose retorted. "*Not* my choice, by the way, as you well know. Your father ran out on us. I had fourteen years with my David before he died. If you're still married by Christmas, whether you claim you were motivated by love or whatever else, *then* I'll listen to your views on the subject, honey!"

"And I'll be happy to give them to you, Mom," Suzanne said through clenched teeth.

Awkward silence.

"Well, as I said, congratulations," Michael Feldman repeated.

Suzanne looked hot, unhappy, frustrated, angry and at the end of her—rapidly fraying—rope. Her skin was papery with fatigue, and her eyes were pink-rimmed and dry. After what she'd put herself through for the past couple of months, she seemed to have no strategy left for dealing with her difficult mother.

It was the wrong time to step in and explain anything to Dr. Feldman, Stephen decided. That would need a delicacy and mastery that Suzanne wasn't showing, and which he wasn't confident he possessed right now, either.

"Michael, can we make a time to meet next week?" he said quietly. "I need to talk to you about a couple of things."

"Yes, of course."

"Now I'm going to take my wife home," he announced, slipping an arm around her waist. He felt the gust of shuddery breath she let out. "She's exhausted, and I'm worried about her."

"Going to put her to bed?" Rose asked.

"That's exactly what I'm going to do." He refused to rise to the double meaning in her words. Suzanne shifted against him like a nervous horse trying to slip its halter, but he wasn't letting her go. She needed this. She needed his strength, and he wanted to give it to her.

"Give me your phone number, honey," Rose ordered, turning to her daughter.

"Sure. Uh, Stephen, do you have it?"

He scribbled it down for her on some scrap paper provided by Terri.

In the elevator, as soon as they were alone, however, he couldn't quite keep the anger out of his voice as he asked Suzanne, "Why didn't you fight? You could hardly have come across less sympathetically if you'd tried!"

She looked miserable and sick about the whole scene, but she wasn't going to take his outspoken criticism lying down. He knew it as soon as she lifted her chin.

"I can't fight, okay?" she said. "I can never win a fight like this with Mom. She always puts the opposite spin on things from what I expect. Like that stuff about love at first sight, tonight! It's like trying to hold on to a handful of Jell-O. She always catches me on the wrong foot. I get paralyzed. Self-conscious. Clumsy. Hostile. You saw it, didn't you? Don't ask me to change in an instant, when I've been trying to do it my whole adult life."

"There's a lot at stake," he pointed out.

The elevator began to skim them noisily toward street level.

"Don't tell me that as if I don't know it! I *know* it, Stephen, believe me. But Mom has done this to me since I can remember. I can't count how many times as a child I ended up confessing to things I hadn't done, purely because of how she reacted. Taking the last cookies from the jar. Leaving a wet towel on the couch. Yes, okay, I did it all! And in my teens, when boys started calling…"

Her voice was low and fast and shaking with emotion. The elevator doors opened and she hurried out, scarcely breaking her flow.

"You know, some embarrassed seventeen-year-old

would come into the house while I was still—of course!—panicking in front of the mirror upstairs. Mom would give him this stuff about not treating her daughter wrong or, worse, gush about how I never stopped talking about him and she could feel major romance in the air. One way or the other, she'd scare the pants off him. She used her own charm, too. I think she might even have come on to a couple of them. I didn't know what she was doing until Jill and Catrina got old enough to understand it and tell me about it. I always thought it was my fault when no boy ever asked me out twice."

"You're stronger than that now."

"Yes," she agreed. "I am. But not when Mom's around. It's too ingrained. She sends me straight back to the old patterns."

"Why do you still have anything to do with her?"

"Because she's my mother."

Her angular body language told him very clearly that she didn't want to talk about it anymore, and they were both left in a state of frustration. Stephen wanted to tell her that those old patterns could be broken, but he knew it would take more than a few words from him.

What's it going to take for you to recognize your own power, Suzanne? I need you to be strong. I've still got so much more to ask of you. Don't let me down.

But he knew it would be far too dangerous to say these words tonight, so he was silent, just as she was.

When they were out in the street, he asked, "Shall we take a cab this time?"

"The subway's fine. Probably quicker. I really don't care."

Suzanne knew she'd angered Stephen tonight. Disappointed him, too. He'd wanted a far better fight from her.

"Yeah, well, join the club," she muttered to herself. He was right. She had proved her own strength in so many ways. But not with Rose. Not yet.

"Are you trying to shake me off your tail, Suzanne?" he said behind her, a few moments later.

"I'm not walking that fast!" she snapped over her shoulder.

He shrugged. "Okay. We can jog, if you like."

"No, thanks!"

"I'm sorry that I was angry, Suzanne."

"That makes one of us!"

"With me? You're *not* sorry you're angry, and you're angry with me?"

"It's a fifty-fifty split. With you. With myself. Do you think I don't wish I had a better strategy with Mom? Of course I do!"

"You'll wish it harder if you lose Alice."

"Stop telling me things I already know!"

She ducked down the grimy steps of the subway entrance, got a piece of freshly discarded gum stuck to her shoe and the shoe came off. She darted back for it, glaring at him on the way, daring him to go and rescue the shoe on her behalf. No, thanks! She wasn't that helpless!

But when she pulled it off the filthy cement, half the gum came with it. The tissue she took from her pocket was completely useless in getting it off, and she didn't want to gum up her keys by using one of those.

It was one of those last-straw type situations that wouldn't have bothered her on a good day. This, her wedding day, was no longer a good day.

"Okay, *now* I'll accept your help and your advice," she told him. "How do I get this cursed stuff off?"

"Well, possibly this is the reason I'm still carrying around the expired gasoline credit card I had for two years when I was studying here," he answered.

He took his wallet from his pocket, found the card among a sheaf of others and used its sturdy edge to scrape the gum away. When it was all stuck to plastic instead of shoe, he tossed card and gum into a garbage can.

A couple of aggressive-looking teens passed them on the subway steps, eyeing the wallet still in Stephen's hand. They hesitated for a second, then moved on ahead. Suzanne realized it was the first time in her adult life she'd had a man beside her who was strong enough, imposing enough, to make a moment like that into something unthreatening and quickly over with.

I could get used to this. It was a pity his strength wasn't something she could borrow, like a coat on a cold night.

Only as the train was slowing at their stop did she think to ask him, "So why *do* you still carry an expired gasoline credit card around in your wallet, Stephen?"

"Good memories," he said. "At one time, it seemed likely I'd stay here."

"At one time? I thought—"

"Yes," he interjected quickly. "Once again, it's looking as though that could happen."

"You'd be pleased if it did, then?"

"I want what's best for Alice. I guess that's what I was really nostalgic for, when I kept that card. For a time when I only had to think about what was best for me."

"Everyone has to leave that time behind," she said. "Some sooner than others. It's like the vacations you take as a kid. You can't take those vacations once you grow up. Even if you do go back to that little cabin on the lake, it's not the same."

"True. But I think we're allowed to keep a few souvenirs."

"I'd say we're foolish if we don't."

"What have you kept, Suzanne? From the vacations you took as a child?"

They were still talking about it when they reached the apartment. It was a whimsical subject. Safe. Unchallenging. So few of their conversations had been without some deeper intent that Stephen enjoyed this one a lot more than he probably should have.

It would be so easy to let down his guard. He'd almost slipped earlier, speaking as if a permanent future in the United States was something he no longer considered possible, even though he knew how much Suzanne was hoping he'd start to make plans in that direction. What he'd ended up telling her—that it "could happen"—amounted to a lie, and it nagged at him, souring his gut.

He had no intention of staying here. It just wasn't possible.

But he couldn't afford to develop a hair-trigger conscience about the half truths and generalizations he was fobbing her off with. She would understand eventually, he hoped, and that would have to be good enough for both of them.

What if she *didn't* understand?

He didn't want to think about this possibility. He'd staked Alice's whole future on linking himself with Suzanne. Had that been a mistake? Should he have looked longer and harder at what he could have achieved through greedy Rose, by aligning himself with her claim? Or could he have ignored personalities completely and gone straight to the diplomatic arena?

Dear lord, he was tired, too, that was part of the problem. Nearly as tired as Suzanne.

"It's not that late," she said. "But I'm going to bed."

Zing! Just the mention of the word sent a vibration through the air between them.

Tonight, he thought. She wouldn't turn me down, I'm sure of it, and it would bind her to me in a way that nothing else could. She'd go with me willingly then, wouldn't she, when it came time to take Alice to Aragovia?

Suzanne was wandering across the huge expanse of carpet toward the master bedroom, but she had hesitated, stopping to examine an ornament. Waiting for him to make a move? She had a far softer pink in her cheeks, now, than the hot, self-conscious color she'd worn during and after that awkward scene with her mother and Michael Feldman.

FREE BOOKS! FREE GIFT!

PLAY BANGO!

AND CLAIM 2 FREE BOOKS AND A FREE GIFT!

BANGO

5	19	32	54	73
6	17	41	50	6
13	22	FREE	52	
5	24	44	46	
8	21	35	47	75

BANGO

9	19	44	52	71
4	20	32	50	68
11	18	FREE	53	63
7	27	36	60	72
3	28	41	47	64

BANGO

38	9	44	10	38
92	7	5	27	14
2	51	FREE	91	67
75	3	12	20	13
6	15	26	50	31

★ **No Cost!**
★ **No Obligation to Buy!**
★ **No Purchase Necessary!**

TURN THE PAGE TO PLAY ➡

PLAY BANGO!

AND GET THREE FREE GIFTS!

It looks like BINGO, it plays like BINGO but it's FREE

HOW TO PLAY:

1. With a coin, scratch the Caller Card to reveal your 5 lucky numbers and see that they match your Bango Card. Then check the claim chart to discover what we have for you — 2 FREE BOOKS and a FREE GIFT — ALL YOURS, ALL FREE!

2. Send back the Bango card and you'll receive two brand-new Silhouette Romance® novels. These books have a cover price of $3.99 each in the U.S. and $4.50 each in Canada, but they are yours to keep absolutely free.

3. There's no catch. You're under no obligation to buy anything. We charge nothing — ZERO — for your first shipment. And you don't have to make any minimum number of purchases — not even one!

4. The fact is, thousands of readers enjoy receiving our books by mail from the Silhouette Reader Service™. They enjoy the convenience of home delivery…they like getting the best new novels at discount prices, BEFORE they're available in stores…and they love their *Heart to Heart* subscriber newsletter featuring author news, horoscopes, recipes, book reviews and much more!

5. We hope that after receiving your free books you'll want to remain a subscriber. But the choice is yours — to continue or cancel, any time at all! So why not take us up on our invitation, with no risk of any kind. You'll be glad you did!

YOURS FREE!

**This exciting mystery gift
is yours free when you
play BANGO!**

Visit us online at
www.eHarlequin.com

It's fun, and we're giving away
FREE GIFTS
to all players!

PLAY BANGO!

CALLER CARD

SCRATCH HERE!

YES! Please send me the 2 free books and the gift for which I qualify! I understand that I am under no obligation to purchase any books as explained on the back of this card.

YOUR CARD ↘

BANGO

38	9	44	10	38
92	7	5	27	14
2	51	FREE	91	67
75	3	12	20	13
6	15	26	50	31

CLAIM CHART!

Match 5 numbers	2 FREE BOOKS & A MYSTERY GIFT
Match 4 numbers	2 FREE BOOKS
Match 3 numbers	1 FREE BOOK

315 SDL DFUF

(S-R-OS-01/02)
215 SDL DFUG

NAME (PLEASE PRINT CLEARLY)

ADDRESS

APT.#   CITY

STATE/PROV.   ZIP/POSTAL CODE

Offer limited to one per household and not valid to current Silhouette Romance® subscribers.
All orders subject to approval.

The Silhouette Reader Service™ — Here's how it works:

If offer card is missing write to: Silhouette Reader Service, 3010 Walden Ave., P.O. Box 1867, Buffalo, NY 14240-1867

BUSINESS REPLY MAIL
FIRST-CLASS MAIL   PERMIT NO. 717-003   BUFFALO, NY

POSTAGE WILL BE PAID BY ADDRESSEE

SILHOUETTE READER SERVICE
3010 WALDEN AVE
PO BOX 1867
BUFFALO NY 14240-9952

NO POSTAGE
NECESSARY
IF MAILED
IN THE
UNITED STATES

All he had to do was walk across the room and gather her into his arms. All he had to do...

Yes. *Yes.*

She made a tiny sound in her throat as she nestled against him, seconds later. He couldn't see her face, because she was staring down. Her hair was brushing the hollow beside his shoulder. He stroked the back of her head. They were both a little awkward. Awed.

He was. She felt so right, like the last piece of a puzzle slotting into place. He hadn't expected it. He hadn't been looking for it at all, two weeks ago, when he'd made the long series of flights from Aragovia's tiny Bersau Airport, via Prague and London, to New York. He'd told his advisers that even the most cold-blooded political marriage would have to wait until he was ready, and now he had a wife whom he longed to take to bed.

He couldn't pinpoint the moment he'd decided to go to her, just now. His legs had moved on their own, and he was there before he knew he'd moved. He was there, holding her, touching his lips to her hair and her face, slow-dancing his tongue in her mouth. He loved the way she clung to him, as if her body were taking her on a ride that scared and exhilarated her beyond anything in her previous experience.

"Yes," he told her, exulting in her need. "Hold me. Don't let go."

"I won't. I'm not planning to."

She was leading him to the bedroom, backing toward the white-and-gold-paneled door, pulling his hands with hers, kissing him as they went. Long, bold, sensuous kisses, openmouthed, exploratory, *sure.* He could feel the hunger in her, and the impatience, and there was something utterly delicious about it when he contrasted it with the innocence she so often betrayed.

The innocence.

He remembered what she'd said about her mother and those teenage boys tonight. She must have spent years doubting herself, and yet she was so beautiful.

"No, stop," he said suddenly. "Stop, Suzanne."

He took her shoulders and pushed her away, holding her at arm's length. Her eyes were dark and wide with desire, and he could see the peaks of her nipples as tight as spring buds through her thin sweater.

"I thought—" Suddenly, she was uncertain. She could hardly focus her gaze, and her mouth looked pink and swollen. Hardly surprising, since his own lips were half-numbed.

How the hell was he going to explain this without hurting her, adding to those old, deep wounds that Rose had made?

How about the truth?

Sorry, Suzanne, I want you, too, but I've just had a very inconvenient crisis of conscience and I'm not going to use the power of lovemaking to get you where I need you to be. Well, not yet, anyway. I'm going to wait until I've thoroughly seduced your heart before I tackle your body.

Revulsion came on him like a high fever, and he hated himself. Hated his country, too. Ached with bitter longing for a time when he'd felt like Jodie and her father and had thought he could turn his back on six hundred years of his family's history, six hundred years when his ancestors had held the Aragovian people's happiness in their hands.

But he'd learned four years ago that for him it wasn't possible, that there was a need, deep in his blood, to serve Aragovia or die trying. That was when he'd turned his back on a lucrative medical career in the United States and had returned home. Then, he had accepted Aragovia's pull on him willingly. Now, Suzanne's pull in the opposite direction was getting stronger all the time.

"Stephen?" she said uncertainly.

"I'm sorry. It's not your fault."

He wheeled away from her so that she wouldn't see his naked struggle to regain control.

"I didn't think it was," she said quickly, her voice firm and steady. She added more honestly, "I didn't *want* to think it was. It's yours, apparently, and I'd like to know why."

"It's...too soon." He sounded like a blushing Victorian bride. Wouldn't have blamed her if she'd laughed.

But she didn't. Instead, she flushed, and her self-doubt changed direction, like one of Rose's attacks. "I— Perhaps you think American women are far too—"

"No. *No!* Too honest about their bodies and their needs? No! You mustn't think that. Too eager to talk? That, I'll agree with. Must we analyze any of this? Pull it apart like this?"

He felt imprisoned by the need to explain, but it was a problem of conscience more than gender.

Once more, I'm hiding behind the easy statements I know she'll accept. Once more, I'm lying to her....

"All right." She nodded. Her arms were folded across her chest now, lifting her full breasts a little, but hiding those telltale nipples. ''Good night, then, Stephen.''

''Good night.'' It wasn't enough. He had to offer her more than that, and this time something safe and good, without a hidden meaning. ''Tomorrow we'll shop for Alice?'' he said, and got his reward.

She smiled, and a glint of mischief and delight appeared in her eyes. It made her more beautiful than ever. ''That's when you'll find out about an American woman's needs,'' she said. ''When she goes shopping!''

''I can't wait,'' he answered, and discovered that he meant it.

Chapter Six

"I like to see a woman with adventure in her blood," Stephen commented the next day. They'd already been shopping for several hours. "You do like new things."

Suzanne had to blush. Until now, she had budgeted so carefully for Alice's homecoming. She'd put away some money each week since finding the library job. This had meant some scrupulous saving, but that hadn't mattered. She just was *not* willing to regard the baby's trust fund as her own personal limitless credit card, the way Rose was so eager to do.

But when Stephen insisted that he should be allowed to contribute, the careful budget suddenly got a whole lot roomier.

Whoo-hoo! Stand aside, everyone. There's a woman on the loose, with intent to shop.

She had been pulled this way and that by so many deep emotions over the past couple of months. There was her initial fear that Alice wouldn't survive at all. There was the sense of loss and grief for a half sister she would never have the chance to get to know. There was love for a baby which she couldn't yet express through hugging and tickling and finger games. And she was yearning to hug and kiss Alice so much, instead of holding her like a piece of fragile glass.

All of it crystallized into a spending frenzy she never would have allowed herself without Stephen's encouragement.

"You're *making* me get this baby swing," she said.

"We need something to fill up that apartment."

"And the mobile?"

"It attaches to the side of her crib, see? It plays 'Lara's Theme' from *Dr. Zhivago*."

"And this dress? It's fit for a princess! Oh! Right!"

"I thought that maybe," he answered gently, "just *one* dress fit for a princess, under the circumstances, wouldn't be too out of line."

"She's always been a princess to me." Suzanne hugged the tiny lilac silk and lace dress against her cheek and touched the tip of her finger to one of the tiny cream silk rosebuds at its waist. She ached for there to be a real baby Alice, cooing and laughing, inside the little dress. "I don't care about the technicalities, and I'm glad it's not really relevant anymore."

"Why is that?" he asked.

"Well, wouldn't it be horrible if she had to grow up under a microscope, like the British royal family, with cameras clicking in her face all the time, and never any chance to be a real child?"

He gave a tiny nod. "Of course. But Aragovia's not like that. I would never permit any of that for her."

He sounded stiff and she shot him a curious look, a little surprised that he seemed to have taken offense. "I'm sorry," she said quickly. "That wasn't a criticism of you."

Why on earth should he interpret it as one?

"No," he answered, his frown clearing. "No, of course it wasn't. Did you decide on getting this little playsuit?" he added quickly.

He held it up, but she shook her head. "The ones we saw in the other store were just as good, and half the price. This...uh...probably isn't good for me, Stephen," she added. "I've never spent money like this before in my life, and I think it's going to my head. I feel kind of light and floaty."

"The fact that we skipped lunch might also have something to do with that."

She grinned. "Okay, so I didn't want to stop shopping in order to eat, in case all the stores suddenly sold out of their entire range of baby things. I hope you're not telling me that was paranoid?"

"Are you happy with what we've bought?"

"I'm—" she took a deep breath and felt her throat tighten and her eyes fill with tears "—just happy to have her to shop for. Even if I could have afforded it earlier, I wouldn't have dared to do it until I heard the verdict on her discharge yesterday. Because of her health, because of all sorts of things. But today, knowing her crib and dresser and change table are being delivered on Monday, and having all these bags

and packages to carry home, at last I'm starting to
believe that it's real.''

"Yes, it's real," he echoed softly.

"That the feed tube and the mask and the alarm
and the monitor lines are going to disappear pretty
soon, and I'll be able to hold her whenever I want.
Not *prepare* for it, like a military exercise, the way
it is when I hold her now. Truthfully, I wouldn't have
cared if she had to sleep in a drawer lined with blankets, and wear charity store hand-me-downs.''

"Well, I guess we could return all of this."

"Just try!"

They were still laughing when they reached the
apartment, filling the marble-floored entrance hall
with a litter of bags and boxes. It was five in the
afternoon by this time, and Stephen was right. Despite
the substantial rolls he had bought for their late break-
fast, she shouldn't have skipped lunch.

"I ordered dinner for eight-thirty," he said. "But
we should have something now as well. Why don't
you take care of the shopping while I see what Arkady and Sonia have in their kitchen.''

Wrapped up in an orgy of tag snipping, Suzanne
hardly heard him. "Mm, nice," she agreed automatically. The little stretchy pastel playsuits with the
smocking across the front were so adorable. And the
plush moose had such soft fur, and such a serious
moosey face.

She was still dealing with the tiny clothes and won-
dering if the diaper bag was too big when she heard
him behind her and felt the cold press of a tall glass
in her hand.

"What's this?"

"Arkady and Sonia seem to have stocked up on foods beginning with the letter *C*," he answered. "It's champagne. I've also managed to put together a platter of caviar, crackers and camembert cheese. Apart from oatmeal and some tiny pots of English marmalade, it was all I could find."

"I guess water doesn't begin with the letter *C*. Too bad!"

"The champagne is for a toast, Suzanne," he said patiently.

"Do we need a toast?"

"We do. To playsuits and plush mooses!" He put the platter of foods-beginning-with-*C* on the hall table and held his glass high.

"Okay, you're right." Suzanne stood up, grinning. "And diapers and baby lotion," she responded.

"And no more feed tube and monitors."

"But night feeds and teething troubles instead."

"And to the two of us, because we've done this for her, and we're going to make it work."

They clinked their champagne flutes together and drank, and the bubbly, straw-colored liquid paused briefly in Suzanne's empty stomach then went straight to her head. A teaspoon of caviar on a cracker wasn't anywhere near enough to soak it up. The marble floor, still covered in shopping bags, rolled gently beneath her feet and she felt very, very happy and teetering deliciously on the brink of love.

She was totally confident, too, about the response she would get when she snuggled herself dreamily into Stephen's arms, and she wasn't wrong.

"I can't fight this anymore, Suzanne," he said, his voice rough with need.

"I don't want you to." She felt the knots in his muscles and shifted sinuously in his arms to try to ease the knots away. "Can't you understand that?"

"But I should fight it."

"No. Why? You said that it would be obvious if the right time came, and it is. It's what we want. And what could be better for showing Dr. Feldman that we're united, and that we can successfully make a family for Alice? The fact that we've found this together."

She didn't care that her words were a little fuzzy. Didn't even think that it was the champagne. She'd only had half a glass. It was Stephen himself, and his effect on her senses.

"Suzanne…" He was kissing her, his mouth still sweet and tingling from the champagne, his fingers cold against her face from touching the chilled flutes. "I can't say no to it."

"Don't say no. I don't want you to," she repeated.

He dragged his mouth from hers, held her face in his hands, gave her one suffering look and answered, "All right. Yes. All right."

He swept her into his arms and carried her to the bedroom, his hot blue gaze locked with hers the whole way, as if he were daring her to protest. But protest was the furthest thing from her mind. It was delicious and fabulous to have her own inner desire translated into his confident actions.

She had initiated this, just now, but he had taken over, wearing his previous experience like a well-cut suit. His smile tucked in one corner of his mouth as he dumped her with a single sweeping movement onto the bed. Its soft, luxurious depths cushioned her as she shamelessly watched him undress.

First came the casual pale gray sweater, pulled off in a couple of fast, impatient movements. His stomach was so firm and flat you could have balanced one of those champagne flutes on it. Next, he prised off his running shoes with their laces still tied, like a ten-year-old boy.

"So is this a one-man show?" he asked, running a hot gaze down her body, which was still fully clothed.

"I hope not...."

The teasing, slightly imperfect smile was still in place as he pulled her shoes off, then engulfed her feet in the grip of hands that were suddenly hot. No man had ever caressed her feet before. He stroked and kneaded and held them, then moved higher to her calves, every movement telling her in terms she couldn't mistake, *This is what I'm going to do to the rest of your body, too.*

Unable to hide her pleasure, she watched what the action of his hands did to the muscles of his upper arms and chest, then couldn't drag her eyes away as his fingers moved to the fastening of his jeans.

Unashamed of his nakedness, he strode across to close the cream damask drapes, making the room shadowy in the late-afternoon light. It was dark enough to soften the newness of this, yet light enough for her to see the hunger in his face. He slid the silky fullness of her skirt up to her thighs, stroked the sensitive inner skin, then a moment later got his fingers tangled in the buttons of her blouse and laughed at his own clumsiness.

"Excuse me. This is the only part I'm not good at."

"No, you're good at this, too," she whispered, because the heels of his hands were touching the fullness of her breasts with such soft caresses, as he worked on the buttons, that she could hardly breathe.

He reached around to unfasten her bra, then slid the straps from her shoulders and flung the garment aside. She heard the inward hiss of his breath as he cupped her. Her control rapidly fraying, she arched to meet his touch, then moaned with impatience and pulled his head down to her mouth.

He kissed her, with a blend of hunger and sweetness that was like the contrast of ice cream and hot fudge sauce, and she moved her hands wantonly on his body, touching him, exploring him, arousing him. She hadn't known that she possessed this exquisitely feminine power. Now, suddenly, she was giddy and exultant with it.

She could make him moan and shudder. She could roll him over, stretch herself on top of him and watch as he threw his head back in ecstasy and need. She could make his eyelids quiver and the breath pant in and out of his mouth. She could tease him, steal soft, juicy kisses, then take her mouth away from his so that he came seeking her, wanting her back. She could brush her nipples deliberately against his chest so that his hands tightened convulsively against her upper thighs.

"Suzanne, please!" he begged.

She laughed. "Patience..."

"No..." He gave a growl that was both fierce and amused. "I have no patience at all!"

He rolled again, and he was on top this time. At first she thought he'd meant what he'd said—that he was ready and relentless and wouldn't wait. At the thought of it, she felt a throbbing, deep inside her, of both apprehension and expectancy. How would it feel to have him sweep to fulfillment like a flood tide, blind, unheeding and unstoppable? Would it be pain or pleasure?

But then, as he looked down at her, he suddenly went still, as if frozen by something he saw in her eyes. "You're so beautiful," he whispered, tracing a finger across the line of her lips and up to the sensitive skin just above her cheekbones. "We must make this perfect, tonight..."

Nothing made much sense after that. The clumsiness of her sketchy previous experience hadn't prepared her for such a total, blissful disorientation. From somewhere, he produced a foil packet. There was a little pain, soon eased away. There was the warmth of his weight, the tumble of dark patterns behind her closed eyes, the rhythm of breathing, the whisper of words and an ecstasy that was utterly new. They arrived at the crest of the wave together. It broke, sending them both tumbling into a place where nothing else existed but this.

When they lay still afterward, she was so happy that she couldn't speak, and that didn't matter, because he'd fallen into a light doze, his head pillowed on her shoulder and his hand cradling her breast. He seemed oddly vulnerable at that moment, entrusting his body to her while he slept.

She touched his hair, ran her fingers lightly down

his spine and he awoke again almost at once, already smiling.

"What could we do next, I wonder?" he whispered.

"Something has made me very, very hungry," Suzanne said.

"It was the shopping," he answered. He loved the wickedness in her face. He had half feared an evening of watching her in silent thought, or even remorse, but this mischief was an unexpected treat.

"We've been eating since, oh, about six o'clock," she said.

"I think we started eating a little later than that."

"Mm, I guess my perception of time got a bit fluid at one stage." She looked self-conscious and happy and shy and still wicked, all at once.

It was now nine-thirty, and they were just finishing the three-course honeymoon meal that Stephen had ordered in from a restaurant recommended by Arkady and Sonia Radouleau.

"Finish that last profiterole, Suzanne," he suggested.

She took it obediently, opened her mouth and grinned. "Gee, it's such a hardship to obey an order like that!" Then she returned to what they'd been talking about before.

"So your father was how much older than Jodie's dad?" she asked.

He had been telling her more about his family as they ate—about his great-grandparents' long and happy marriage, about his grandfather's death at Stalingrad in 1943 and his father's tragic loss in the Soviet Afghanistan campaign in 1979. The subject had

come up naturally—he couldn't remember exactly
how—but he knew that it was time he opened to her
a little more in any case.

How much more? Put that decision in the too hard
basket!

"He wasn't older," he answered her. "My father
was younger than Alex by five years."

"Funny, I wonder why I had the opposite impression," she said innocently.

There was a small silence, the first note of awk-
wardness between them all day.

I could let it go, Stephen knew. *I could still let it
go so easily. It's such a small point. She won't make
the connection that the question of who was the elder
brother has made a vital difference to Alice's future.*

Yes, and there was a reason why she wouldn't
make such a connection. He hadn't given her any of
the facts she needed to work with. He stared that un-
pleasant little truth in the face for a long moment,
then knew what he had to do. The clock on the ticking
time bomb of his conscience had just run out.

"There's something you need to know, Suzanne,"
he said, speaking with unusual deliberation after the
ease and happiness between them today. "It's time I
told you. And it's complicated. Can you listen carefully?"

"Of course."

"There has been a national vote in Aragovia, and
my family has been asked to return to the throne."

"Your family? To rule again?" She was alert at
once.

She's far more intelligent than Rose, he realized.
Why doesn't she understand that that makes her
stronger as well?

"So the fact that you're a prince *does* matter," she went on. "You told me it didn't. Dear lord, why didn't I do my research on this? Why did I let Alice's needs blind me? I should have realized your willingness was too convenient. You've been able to play it exactly the way you wanted to."

"I...didn't want to frighten you off," he admitted. "But yes, it matters. The ceremonial head of state in the new democratic government is to be the closest heir by blood, whether male or female, to the last ruling prince."

"The last ruling prince. That was Peter Christian," she answered, nodding. Again her mind had moved quickly, but she held her body cautiously. "Yes, all right, you've told me about him. And the closest heir, presumably, is—"

She stopped and froze, and Stephen saw the exact moment of full understanding etched onto her face. The delicate half-eaten profiterole crushed in her fingers, covering them in chocolate and cream, but she didn't seem to notice.

"No, it's *not* you, is it?" she said in a strained voice. "It's Alice. *It's Alice.* But Stephen...dear God...that changes everything!"

"Yes, it does," he said quickly. This was the moment where he would lose her, he knew, if he wasn't careful, and a full explanation seemed like the only course to take. Had he won her over enough, shopping with her, making love to her? Their powerful connection was accidental. Would she still accept that it was real?

"It's vitally important," he continued. "She must grow up in the Aragovian tradition. The old court protocols are being examined and discussed even now." He knew he was speaking with too much urgency, tried to rein it in but without much success. As with Suzanne in her dealings with her mother, understanding of his response did not bring control over it. "I will act as regent on her behalf, ruling in her place until she reaches eighteen. Then she will take the throne in her own right, but she *must* be prepared."

"Prepared... How?"

"I want to take her back with me as soon as possible, to be raised in my country. It's the only way. She *must* have the support of the people, as well as a deep-seated understanding of her duties and her role. To be honest, too, the country needs her inheritance. There's so much we need to rebuild. The education system is poor, the infrastructure in some parts of the country is almost nonexistent. We must step in quickly and show that the new government is strong, proactive and untainted by corruption."

"Stop! Just stop, right now! This is—" Suzanne stood up, wiped the cream and chocolate roughly from her fingers and went to the window that overlooked Fifth Avenue.

From where Stephen sat, he could see the red taillights of traffic that still moved south toward midtown in a steady stream, but he could tell that the sight was only a blur to Suzanne.

"I'm not stupid," she said, as if she was talking to herself. "I haven't misunderstood this, have I?"

Then she turned.

"You've lied to me. You've *used* me!" Her voice cracked. "I'm not wrong! You came over here, with this agenda in place from the beginning, knowing *from the beginning* that you wanted to take Alice away. Take her away from me. To turn her into something *you* think she should be. To take her to a country her own mother and grandfather had rejected—''

''Because they saw no future there. There *is* a future for her there now! And I'm not planning to take her away from you. Of course I'm not! You see, I'd hoped—''

But she wasn't listening anymore. ''*This* is 'the Aragovian thing.' It's very recent, then. Even Dr. Feldman doesn't know the whole story.''

It wasn't a question, but he answered it anyway. ''Very recent, yes. The final vote was taken, to choose between three different models for government, just a few days before I came here. On January first next year, the new constitution will come into effect. Only one of those models included the restoration of my family to the throne. I had to wait until the count was completed before I could leave. We had no idea how close it was going to be, or which model the people would choose.''

''What, no exit polls?''

''Not in Aragovia.''

''Stand-over tactics, then? Voter intimidation?''

''Sadly, my supporters didn't have the resources for those.'' His sarcasm bit hard, and he was angry that she had chosen to see all of this in the worst possible light. Angry only with her? Or with himself as well? ''But in fact,'' he continued, ''there was a large majority in favor of our plan. Stand-over tactics would not have been necessary.''

''If you'd been voted down, you wouldn't have come, because you wouldn't have needed Alice.''

''Yes, I would still have come.''

''Why? You wouldn't have needed her!''

"I would still have come," he repeated.

"Why?"

"To see her. To send that little pink bootie back to my mother."

"Don't!" She said it as if he had struck her. "That was the first moment when I thought—" She began again. "That was the *one thing* that made me trust you. Don't think that you had me won over so easily that first day! I knew there was more to this. But then you talked about your mother's feelings, and I was sure you meant what you said. Was that just a strategic move, too?"

"No. I wouldn't have lied to you about that."

"But you lied to me about other things. You used me!"

Suzanne's throat hurt with the effort of pushing speech past the tension that clamped it like a strong hand. Just a few hours ago, she had made love with him, slept with him. It had been magic. It had changed her. And maybe if she hadn't done it, she wouldn't be feeling such a deep running sense of betrayal.

"I—I knew there was something," she said. Her fingers twisted together in agitation. "That first day we met, once or twice, I had the sense that you were calculating something, hiding something. After that...I lost that perception. Other things got in the way."

Like their powerful shared attraction. Was it really shared? Or was that only a part of his strategy as well?

She doubted everything about him, now. He was seven years older than she was, and more experienced in every way. He could have faked every second of his response to her. A man didn't have to care deeply about a woman to have the physical ability to make love to her. He could have consciously worked at switching on her need for him, hoping it would soften her like wax in his hands.

And, oh, she had been like wax! Hot and responsive and pliable beneath his touch. Flaming like a candle.

"I didn't want you to react this way, Suzanne," he said.

"No, I don't imagine you did. I expect you wanted—and maybe you were quite sure I would do it!—wanted me to say, 'Yes, sweetheart. Whatever you want, sweetheart. Now that you've made love to me, I'll happily let you spirit Alice out of the country.' Maybe if I'm lucky, you'll even let me visit her occasionally, as long as I don't object to all the correct court protocols, and as long as I walk nine paces behind her gilded ceremonial state stroller at all times. That's not what I want for her! This is worse than what Mom and Perry have planned. And you were totally wrong to think you could seduce me into giving it to you!"

She stormed out of the room, knew he would follow her, and didn't care. If he thought he could stop her, talk her out of this, sweet-talk her or kiss her out of this, he was dead wrong!

"Where are you going?" His voice came urgently from behind her. "Don't leave. This isn't the way you've painted it. That's not how it feels to me. Not anymore."

She grabbed her jacket from the coat stand in the entrance hall, where all the bags of baby things still lay. "I'm going to see Alice. And it kills me that I haven't been today before this. That I've spent the whole day with you, instead of her. It makes me sick.''

She slammed the door behind her. Realized she didn't have a key. Didn't care. She wouldn't be coming back to this apartment. Not ever. She wasn't going to risk getting seduced by its luxury again. She'd go home to that echoey and oddly appealing rehearsal room. There was enough money in her purse for the subway, and that was all that mattered. Seeing Alice was all that mattered.

She felt as if the world were right side up again, after it had sneakily turned itself upside down for a day or two without her noticing. Having her feet well and truly back on the ground might feel a little strange at first, but she knew this was where they really belonged. Taking her to Alice.

She almost ran toward the subway entrance, and ran again from Twenty-Third Street to the hospital.

"Suzanne!" said the baby's nurse for this shift. It wasn't Terri, who didn't work weekends, but another lovely woman called Barbara. "I was afraid we weren't going to see you today."

"Afraid? Why? What's happened to—?" The panicky questions poured out.

"Hey, steady, girl! She's fine. She's doing great. Your mom got to hold her for half an hour, and she just left a little while ago."

"I guess you're too busy to go through the whole holding thing again, right?" Suzanne asked, disappointed. She'd missed out on it yesterday, also, because she found it so impossible to relax when Mom was around.

Mom, Stephen, Feldman... She didn't need all these people, impinging and distracting.

"Honey, no, that's the good news I have for you," Barbara said. "And it's why I was hoping you'd come in. Do you know she's put on 110 grams in the past ten days, with no back-sliding at all? That's nearly four ounces of steady gain. And she's only had three apnea spells since yesterday."

"That's great!"

"Dr. Lewis came by this afternoon and said her chart was looking so good he wanted to try her without the feed tube. She's taken two bottles from me since then, her sucking reflex is working fine and she's keeping most of the feed down. I think he'll okay her for discharge Monday or Tuesday."

"Oh, dear God, she's off the feed tube! Oh, thanks be to God, and I missed it!" Suzanne felt shaky.

"But, honey, it means you can hold her without all the rigmarole. Dr. Lewis says she can go without the oxygen mask and the breathing alarm for short spells, as well, to start weaning her off them. She can just be all swaddled up in a blanket like a regular baby in your arms, for as long as you like."

"Can she really?" It was like Christmas coming three months early, something she needed to hear six times and experience for herself before she'd believe it. "Can I really hold her and hug her and—? Can I feed her, too?"

"Stop talking about it so much, and just do it," Barbara scolded her gently.

"Oh! Oh, this is too good to be true!" Tears came, and she let them flow.

At just over three and a half pounds, Alice was still tiny, like a pink frog, and she'd struggled so hard to almost double her birth weight and reach this size. Cradled in Suzanne's arms, she slept a noisy baby sleep, full of snuffles and squeaks and sucking sounds. Already she had developed watery pink sucking blisters on her lips from her bottle.

The black hair that most premature babies were born with had mostly worn away, now, and in the soft light, Suzanne thought that she could detect the faintest sheen of new growth, this time a pale, silky gold.

"I just know you're going to be a beauty!" she whispered.

My beauty.

Not Mom's little bankroll. Not Aragovia's political pawn. Not Stephen's cosseted, well-prepared princess, either.

My beauty. My baby.

She kissed Alice's soft, scented little head, kissed the dimples at the roots of her fingers, and the little tummy in its cross-over T-shirt and flannel blanket.

But the joy she felt wasn't enough to block out her new understanding that the sense of safety and hope she'd known since yesterday's wedding to Stephen was an illusion. And it was an illusion that Stephen himself had shattered, an hour ago, into a thousand pieces.

Chapter Seven

"Could I have the neonatal unit, please?" Stephen said into the phone.

"Putting you through…"

The phone rang twice and then a woman's voice answered, identifying the name of the unit in a distracted voice.

"This is Stephen Serkin-Rimsky," he said.

"I'm sorry?"

"My cousin, Alice Rimsky, is a patient." He ran his fingers impatiently through his hair. "I'd just like to check that Suzanne arrived there safely a short while ago."

"Yes, she's here. She's holding the baby now. Would you like me to have her come to the phone?"

"No, that's all right, thanks, I just wanted to know that she'd arrived." He'd been concerned at the thought of her traveling alone on the subway this late at night.

He felt empty once he'd put down the phone, with no idea as to what his next move should be.

"Move?" he muttered aloud. "Why am I always thinking in moves? If I hadn't, would she have reacted better? How could I have handled this so she would have reacted better?"

There wasn't a way. Even if he'd been totally upfront from the beginning, so that Suzanne couldn't possibly have made that wild, angry—and truthful?—accusation about his using her, lying to her, and manipulating her feelings, what would have changed? Nothing! Except that probably they wouldn't even have gotten this far. She would never have agreed to marry him at all, and he would have been locked out of the game from the very beginning.

He couldn't have allied himself with Rose. She was too selfish, too manipulative and, he sensed, too much of a loose cannon emotionally. So should he have trusted the courts, or the channels of international diplomacy? That went against the grain of his experience as a doctor.

A victory, even if he achieved one, would take months or even years to eventuate, and would come at the expense of Alice's own well-being. Stephen had seen premature babies before. He'd seen orphaned infants. They needed cherishing, stability and a stress-free environment.

He couldn't have handled this in a way that would have turned Alice into a political commodity, a ward of the court with her future hanging in limbo for months while the Supreme Court decided whether she belonged to Aragovia or to the United States. He couldn't, when at heart, as Suzanne understood, the thing Alice most needed in order to thrive was not Aragovia's crown on her head, but love.

And so he came back to Suzanne. Now that he knew her better, he understood that no matter how he had handled the situation, she would never have accepted the idea that he wanted to spirit Alice away to a distant, unheard of country in order to groom her for her future as Aragovia's ruling princess.

But I'm not planning to spirit her away. I've always hoped that Suzanne would agree to come, too, make our marriage into something we could both respect, for Alice's sake. That "suitable alliance" my advisers want for me has taken on a whole new meaning since we met. Is it possible she doesn't understand that?

He didn't have time to follow the thought through. When the phone rang, he snatched it up, sure that it would be Suzanne herself. Had the nurse given her a message that he'd called? Did she need to speak to him?

But it wasn't Suzanne. It was Rose.

"May I speak to my daughter, please, Stephen?" she said in a honeyed tone, and he was so distracted by the complexity of his feelings that he answered before he thought, "I'm sorry, Rose, she's not here."

"Oh, good grief, it's fallen apart already!"

"She's with Alice at the hospital."

"And why aren't you there with her? Most newlyweds I've had anything to do with are joined at the hip—and other places—on their honeymoon."

He ignored the crude reference to sex. "I've just been on the phone to the unit, to see how they are."

"Which you wouldn't have needed to do if you were there with her."

"You're right, Rose," he agreed smoothly. "I should be with her. She was planning to stay all night, but she needs to rest. If you're suggesting that it's my job to persuade her of that, then, yes, I agree with you completely."

There was a rich laugh at the other end of the phone. "You're cute, Stephen. You remind me of your uncle. But this isn't over yet."

"I wouldn't make the mistake of thinking it was," he said, and pressed his finger down to cut the connection.

He reached the hospital half an hour later. It was almost eleven now, and the unit was about as quiet as a neonatal unit ever got. Where the sickest babies were, the light was still bright because it had to be, to permit doctors and nurses to work safely. At the far end where Alice was, however, it was dimmer.

When Stephen caught sight of Suzanne, his spine tingled. She looked like a holy picture, a *Madonna and Child.* Alice was cradled in her arms, close to her heart, and the light was catching at her hair. So beautiful! It was a very different kind of beauty to the kind she'd radiated in his arms as they made love, but it caught at him just as strongly.

She hadn't seen him yet, because she was gazing down at the baby with a soft look of love on her face, and he took a long moment to look at her, feeling greedy about it.

I don't want her to see me yet. I don't want to break this.

He had to clear his throat before he could speak. She heard the awkward sound and glanced up, and the soft look fled from her expression in an instant, just as he had known it would.

"Your mother called," he said. "If you're planning on abandoning our marriage because of what happened tonight, you may want to reconsider."

"Is that a threat?" she demanded. Her voice was low because of Alice and the other babies and visitors in the unit, but the intensity was stronger than if she'd been shouting. He hated to see her mouth so thin and her eyes so hard. Hated it more because he was the one who had made her look this way.

"No! *Chort vazmi,* how did we get to this point so fast?" He spoke softly, too, but could feel the harshness of his words tightening his throat. He found a second chair and pulled it toward him, scraping the legs with an ugly sound on the vinyl floor.

"You're the one who needs to think about the answer to that question," she said.

"I have thought about it," he answered angrily. "I've thought about little else since you left the apartment. You would have reacted this way no matter when I told you the situation with Alice, whether I'd laid it out like a deck of cards from day one, or whether I'd waited even longer."

"Do you deny that you used me, then? Can you deny that you deliberately gave me the marriage I needed, told me constantly that Alice came first, so that I'd give you what you want?"

"No, I don't deny any of that," he said. "But I didn't lie about what was really important. Alice *does* come first. Her well-being. The love she needs and deserves. That hasn't changed. And at this stage you don't seem to be planning on giving me what I want, so quite frankly everything I've done has been of little benefit!''

He didn't care how cold and careless it sounded. If she wanted honesty, he'd give it to her with a blunt blade.

''You're completely ruthless, aren't you?'' she exclaimed, her voice a hiss. ''Even now, you don't care that you've—''

She stopped, looked down suddenly and began to kiss the baby's head. He guessed that she was fighting tears, and his heart lurched in his chest, making him feel sick to his stomach.

''I care,'' he said roughly. ''I care about Alice, and I care about you. Lord, I don't want to see you so unhappy and angry, Suzanne! Isn't there any way we can work this? I'm not planning to steal her from you. Is that what you think? How could I? Do you think I don't value your love for her? Couldn't you consider that you might make your future in Aragovia, too? That's what I want. Don't you understand?''

''My future in Aragovia? In what role?''

''As her mother, of course.''

''And as your *wife?*'' The word was so bitter on her tongue that he sat back and felt sicker than ever, felt as if he'd bruised her with his own hands, and now she was bruising him back. The idea of their marriage was clearly repugnant to her.

''We can come to any arrangement you like,'' he said, clumsy in his regret. ''My advisers have been telling me for months that it would be better if I were married. You would have many advantages in Aragovia. As Regent, I cannot afford to have a scandalous personal life, but if we were discreet—''

"Discreet affairs? Any arrangement I like?" Her green eyes flashed. "Fine. Great. Easy for you to be generous. Because I'm simply not important, am I? I'm Alice's mother—handy for a baby princess to have a mother. Children seem to have this inconvenient need for love!—but in my own time, I can do what I like. Take up a hobby, maybe. Redecorate my suite. Arrange a few flowers. Have a 'discreet affair' with an ambassador or two."

Stephen hadn't known there could be that much anger in those loving eyes, and suddenly he snapped.

"Has it occurred to you that this cuts both ways?" he demanded. "This stuff about being used? You've used me, too, Suzanne. You needed a husband. You approached the problem with a strength of will and a single-mindedness that bordered on obsession. I was willing, and at the time that was all you wanted to hear."

"That's not true! I asked you what your motivation was, and you told me you were doing it for Alice. Silly me, I took that at face value, didn't ask any more hard questions."

"Perhaps you should have," he said. "I expected questions. You threatened me with them. And then they didn't come."

"I was so happy. For Alice's sake. I believed we were both making the same sacrifice, you and I, with the same hope in our hearts that we could make it work."

"It's a sacrifice which will become useless if we let this issue tear us apart, Suzanne. Your mother is waiting for it to happen, and she's probably right in what she's apparently thinking now—that a hasty

marriage which explodes after a few days will look
far worse to Michael Feldman, and to the family court
judge as well, than if you hadn't married in the first
place.''

''Is that her scenario?''

''From the way she's playing this, yes.''

''Playing it? I *hate* it!''

''I know you do. You're too straightforward to en-
gage in that sort of conniving. I admire that quality
in you, Suzanne.''

''What are you hoping for, when you say things
like that?'' she demanded.

''Nothing. Please don't start assuming that everything I've ever said to you has been motivated by
some hidden goal. Do you want this to reach the point
where the decision must be made by the Supreme
Court? It could happen, if you and I take opposite
positions, and what will that do to Alice?''

But she wasn't prepared to hear it, and he couldn't
blame her for that. He'd destroyed something in her
tonight, something very precious to both of them. For
a long moment, as he looked at her—once more she
was taking refuge in hugging the baby—he wondered
if the price he would have to pay for Aragovia's secure and prosperous future was too high.

Then he thought of the way his people lived, and
of the way he himself had lived until very recently.
Ancient farmhouses with no amenities, or Soviet-style
concrete apartment blocks, dingy, cramped, cracked
and damp. Low wages, poor employment prospects,
systems in service areas such as banking and telecom-
munications that were so cumbersome they barely
functioned at all.

In contrast, he thought of all that the country had to offer. There was the possibility of tourism in its beautiful landscapes, its wine and cheese industries, its sapphire mines and world-class cave systems. The Voltzin Mountains could be developed for winter sports. The lowlands around the Zebruner River would make prime terrain for commercial trout hatcheries. Those ugly Soviet buildings would be pulled down. And this was only the beginning.

There was no reason why Aragovia should remain poor, and the time was ripe for changes to be made *now*, when the people's enthusiasm and optimism were high, church attendance was rising, and investors from Europe and America were eager to step in. Provided, of course, that they were convinced the new form of government was stable.

It has to come first. If I've lost her, destroyed something in her, I regret it deeply, but it cannot sway me. Caring about one woman's feelings, no matter how admirable and true, is a luxury I just don't have. If this falls apart, and there's a divorce, I'll have no choice but to take the question of Alice's future to Rose, a woman I'm coming to despise, or to a diplomatic level, with all the uncertainty and delay that will bring. Can't I convince her that she still needs our marriage?

"Listen," he said, as clearly as he could. "We just can't afford to get distracted with this mistrust. You have to see that. Think about it, and you will. When is Alice to be discharged, have you been told? She must be almost ready."

"Monday or Tuesday," Suzanne answered.

"Then it's very simple. You have until then to decide whether you wish to continue with this marriage."

"It's up to you as well, surely," she retorted. "Why don't you bail out now, and ally yourself with Mom? Tell her she'll get to live in a fairy-tale castle, with servants to wait on her and Perry hand and foot, for the rest of their lives. She and Perry would throw Alice at you like a football, and you could do what you liked with her, if they thought there'd be that much in it for them. Mom's always felt that life owes her a princess's lifestyle, and you could give her one with a snap of your fingers, apparently!"

He ignored her. He could see just how tired and tense and miserable she was, and that she hardly knew what she was saying.

"My decision is made," he said quietly. "It's true that Aragovia needs Alice, but Alice needs you. You love her, and that's crucial. I'm not giving up on our marriage while it still has a chance of keeping the two of you together."

"And I'm not going back to that Fifth Avenue apartment!"

"Then I'll come to you on the West Side."

"Prince Stephen, Regent of Aragovia, living in an unconverted Hell's Kitchen rehearsal space? Oh, puh-lease! It makes even less sense now than it did when I saw you there yesterday, bouncing off those echoing walls! You can't do it!"

"Is that a dare, Suzanne? You weren't planning on staying in that apartment forever. I think we can both wait it out there until the hearing on the custody question. After that, do either of us have the answers?"

"Another one of your stirring speeches, Stephen?"

"Then you don't agree to keeping our marriage alive?"

"Yes, I agree. Of course I agree! What other choice do I have?" Forgetting where she was, her voice rose beyond the low, intense tones they'd both used until now. Another visitor in the unit turned to frown at her, and in her arms tiny Alice awoke and began to cry.

"You don't look happy, Suzie. Don't you think it looks fabulous?"

"Oh, Cat, yes! Yes, it does! I'm sorry, I'm just—"

She stopped. Her stepsister, Catrina Brown, was watching her with a concerned look, and the silence between them was awkward at once. They were both standing in the middle of Suzanne's apartment, which had been transformed during the course of the day.

Cat had potted up a jungle of plants from her cousin Pixie Treloar's garden, and they now sat on the apartment's wide, west-facing sills, soaking up the late sun. She had also brought a big pile of preschool paintings done by Jill's four-year-old, and Suzanne had pinned them on the windowless east wall, creating a splashy mosaic of color for Alice to look at. Strung up in one corner was a stretchy hammock filled with soft toys, many of them gifts to the baby, some of them borrowed from little Sam.

Pixie and her skinny, gallant and ancient boyfriend, Clyde Hammond, were both here as well, and they had spent the day working their magic with fabric and wood. There was still some hammering going on as Clyde finished up, and a whirr from Pixie's industrial-strength sewing machine.

Those heavy drapes were no longer pulled back against the walls like useless black pillars, but had been arranged to divide up the space a little. They were now pulled partway across, looped back in dramatic curves and tied with colorful sashes from Pixie's immense fabric stash. Clyde had made the frames of three large folding screens, which more of Pixie's beautiful fabrics had filled in. She'd even made new silver-gray slipcovers for the couch.

Suzanne had phoned Cat and Pixie yesterday morning, with news of her marriage. She'd stumbled through the story and kept it as brief as she could. For both herself and Stephen, she'd said, it was only about Alice, and that was why she hadn't invited anyone. It had been a very rushed and practical event.

Had she convinced them? She wasn't sure. It was a relief when Cat had quickly moved on to the question of Alice's homecoming and the urgent need to make this apartment more of a home. The response on that issue had been impressive, to say the least.

Cat and Suzanne had just finished arranging the screens so that Alice, Stephen and Suzanne would each have a private place to sleep. If this told everyone more about the state of Suzanne's expedient marriage than she was happy about, then that couldn't be helped. With a big Persian rug, borrowed from Pixie, on the floor, and little touches like a coat stand by the door and pot hooks hung with pans and utensils on the wall above the kitchen sink, the place looked like a home now. There was even a bed for Stephen, brought up from Pixie's in the back of Clyde's pickup.

The place was eccentric, maybe, but it was bright, clean, cozy and welcoming, all the same.

"You're tired, aren't you?" Cat suggested helpfully, after a moment. "And you're nervous about that darling little baby coming home to you as well."

"That's it, I guess," Suzanne agreed.

"And about living here with Stephen?"

"That, too."

Clyde's hammering stopped. "I'd like to meet him," Cat said.

"You will soon, I hope." *Because if it doesn't happen soon, then that will mean we're divorced, and he'll be fighting a legal battle against me to take Alice out of the country. Unless Mom has her...*

"Is he good with Alice?"

"He cares about her a lot."

"Isn't that the only thing that counts?"

No. Not when he's a prince and she's a princess, and their country wants them back.

Suzanne didn't tell Cat, Pixie and Clyde any of this, nor had she told her younger sister, Jill, who was away now.

Half an hour later, the three of them had left. Suzanne tidied up the fabric scraps Pixie had left on the floor and made herself a sandwich. She had stocked the kitchen today, knowing she wouldn't be leaving the apartment very much until Alice was fully settled in. She'd arranged to have the whole of the coming week away from work.

When she was partway through the sandwich, the buzzer by the door made her jump, and then she heard Stephen's voice. "Can I come up?"

"Yes. Okay. I'll buzz you in."

She'd had a key cut for him today. The mundane errand contained an abundance of disturbing symbolism. She pressed the button to release the lock and heard his footsteps on the stairs a short while later. They sounded confident and energetic, and her heart beat faster at the thought of seeing him again.

He was her husband. They'd slept together. Was he her enemy now? Who was betraying whom?

She let him in before he could knock, and felt his physical effect on her, as he came through the wide doorway, like the wall of wind from a bomb blast. It almost knocked her off her feet, and she had to grab the cold edge of Pixie's lacy iron-work table for support.

"Vot... Chudoh!" he said, and it took her a moment to realize he was talking about the apartment. "It's a miracle!"

"My sister and her cousin and a friend came up from Philly. We've been working all day."

"I'd have helped, Suzanne," he said.

"I know. I didn't want you."

He looked at her, his silence challenging her statement better than words could have done. *Is there any point to this?* said his face.

She flushed, and he followed up his advantage. "Do you want to end this now?" he said. "If you do, I can leave. You've had some space to think about it since last night. Tell me if you've changed your mind, and I'll leave now."

"I haven't changed my mind. I need you."

"Then don't punish both of us. Don't punish Alice. If you won't try, this can't work. I was wrong to deceive you. I can see that now. I apologize. We've both been too single-minded about it. Can we start again? Can we learn to trust each other and listen to each other?''

"I don't know, Stephen."

"Try. Or there's no point."

She nodded slowly. "Okay. I'll try."

"Now help me bring up the boxes down in the hall. They are full of my great-grandparents things, and I thought there might be some items we could use."

"I want to go and see Alice soon."

"We'll unpack the boxes when we have time."

"We have Alice's furniture coming tomorrow, and all her clothes and toys to put away. We'll have Alice herself to care for from Tuesday. We may never have time again!"

He laughed at her deliberate humor, and it was the first tentative reaching out between them since things had fallen apart on Saturday night.

"Now, the pediatrician told you, didn't he, that you should probably keep her away from crowds of people for a few more weeks?" Terri said on Tuesday morning, as they prepared for the baby's discharge. "Since Alice couldn't be breastfed, her immune system didn't get that natural boost. Mrs. Wigan, could you excuse me, please?" Terri continued. Rose was resting her hands on the Plexiglas sides of Alice's crib. "We need to get this crib ready for a new admission."

She's always sounded warm toward Mom before, Suzanne realized, but Mom wasn't coming across so well today. She'd never been a patient person, and she didn't enjoy sitting with Alice.

Seeing this clearly, she felt a little more distanced from Rose's usual effect on her today, a little stronger, for some reason.

"Is the car waiting?" she said to Stephen.

"It should be, by now. I ordered it for ten-thirty."

"My goodness! Another limo!" Rose said. "Nice for some!"

Suzanne ignored her, getting nervous about actually taking Alice home at last. The baby's doctor had put her on a daytime program of one hour on oxygen, then one hour off. The equipment, including a breathing mask, was bulky and awkward to handle. Suzanne also knew she mustn't let a naked flame or spark anywhere near the readily combustible oxygen. Despite her familiarity with all this, it was daunting.

"She's waking up," she said, her voice wobbly. "Terri, what if she needs a feed or a change before we get home?"

"You have formula and bottles in her diaper bag, right?" Terri said soothingly. "And she's too little to care about a messy diaper."

"She had that rash last week."

"You have the cream, and you can take her diaper off and let her kick her legs in a patch of sunshine. That'll keep her little bottom nice. Take her to a park."

"I thought you said—"

"Crowds in closed spaces, with heating or air-conditioning, could be a problem," Terri explained. "The park, if it's sunny and warm in the middle of the day, is fine."

"And we hook her up to the tank and mask and alarm as soon as we reach the apartment, right?"

"Honey, stop worrying!"

Terri enfolded Suzanne in a very large, warm hug and there were tears in her eyes when she said, "We'll miss you and that cute baby! We're all so happy that she's going home growing and healthy!"

"I've prayed for it every single day," Rose said.

Terri turned to her. "I've prayed for it, too, Mrs. Wigan. But sometimes praying is the easy part." It was clear that she was thinking about all the hours Suzanne had put in beside the baby's crib.

"Having brought up three daughters, Terri, I know that only too well," Rose agreed. On the surface, her manner was warm, but beneath the veneer neither she nor Terri appeared to be too thrilled with each other.

"Look after her, Mr. Serkin," Terri told Stephen. "Look after both of them. Don't forget this gorgeous doll you brought her from so far away. She tracks its face so beautifully now when she's alert. And let me walk you all to the elevator."

Down in the drop-off area in front of the hospital, Suzanne asked her mother, "Will you come to the apartment with us and help us get her settled?"

"No, but you can run me uptown," Rose answered grudgingly. "Perry and I are checking out today." She looked older, suddenly.

"Oh, you're going back to Philly?"

"No, we're moving somewhere cheaper until this whole thing is settled. You think we can afford to stay on Central Park South forever?" Another change of strategy on Rose's part. She'd belatedly realized how bad it looked for her and Perry to be spending extravagantly on the expectation of Alice's money.

The limousine driver helped Stephen to secure the

infant seat correctly in the vehicle, and commented, "That's a little 'un."

"She'll grow," Suzanne said. The Aragovian doll, nestled in the infant seat beside the baby, was still almost as big as she was.

"Reminds me of my granddaughter," the driver said. "She was tiny, like that. Cute!"

Rose slid into the rear-facing seat, took out a mirror and began to refresh her makeup.

"I should warn you, we'll be well prepared for the hearing with Feldman and the family court representative next week," she said when they reached her hotel. "Don't think that this is over, honey, just because you're taking Alice home with you. You know, I can learn all this special care stuff if I'm given the chance. And there's more than one way to skin a rabbit." Her breathing was a little uneven.

"Mom, you have no idea!" Suzanne muttered.

Fortunately, Rose didn't hear. She climbed carefully out of the car, kissed Suzanne in a cloud of scent and gave a small, rippling wave with four fingers. "We'll see you in court."

"It's not court, Mom."

"It could be, eventually, and don't you forget it!"

"What would you conclude from your mother's threat?" Stephen asked after they had crossed town and pulled up in front of Suzanne's building.

He unclipped the infant carrier and swung it out of the limo, hefting its awkward weight easily. The carrier itself weighed about four times as much as Alice did.

"I wouldn't conclude anything," Suzanne answered him. She took the diaper bag and the oxygen equipment and put both at her feet as she unlocked the front door of the building. Then she turned to Stephen, who was standing beside her. "Mom's changed tack again, and she obviously thinks she's got a lot of cards left up her sleeve, but I'm not going to worry about it. We have Alice to take care of now, and that's enough."

"Good," he said simply, and brushed away a strand of hair that the chilly breeze had blown across her mouth.

For the next three days, Alice set out to prove just how quickly a tiny baby could reduce two capable adults to plates of Jell-O.

She cried, spit up her feeds, got diaper rash, wanted to play in the middle of the night, went to sleep as soon as she got a bottle in her mouth and forgot to finish it. Her apnea alarm went off three or four times a day. It panicked both Stephen and Suzanne, although they both knew what to do, and it usually happened just after one of them had said to the other, "Her apnea alarm hasn't gone off for a good while."

When they had home visits from a specially trained nurse on Wednesday and Thursday, of course, Alice behaved perfectly. She cooed and smiled like a dream and waved her little starfish-shaped hands. As soon as the nurse had left, however, she screamed for an hour, abruptly stopped breathing and triggered her apnea alarm once more.

To sum it all up, she was the prettiest, darlingest Baby from Hell you could possibly hope to meet. The difficult issues between Suzanne and Stephen were shelved for the moment, as they united against a common enemy with far greater power—a preemie baby's needs.

Suzanne got home from picking up milk, bread and eggs on Friday afternoon, the first time she'd been out of the apartment since Tuesday, to find Stephen walking the floor—*again*—with Alice pillowed against his shoulder. She was screaming.

He didn't bother with a greeting, just told her with a hunted look on his face, "You know when I told you I was a family practice specialist, it now seems possible that I only *dreamed* those years of medical training, because this child is certainly not recognizing any of my skills."

"Should we take her out?"

"Out…where?" He blinked blearily, and repeated the words, as if they no longer had any meaning.

He hadn't brushed his hair this morning, hadn't shaved since Monday, and he had a cloth diaper hanging down his back, in completely the wrong spot to be of any use in catching whatever Alice might not want in her tummy. His navy-blue shirt was caught up at the front, showing his flat, tanned stomach and his feet were bare.

Suzanne's heart did a little flip. In a complete mess like this, he still looked gorgeous, and she couldn't stop herself from reaching out to ease the diaper off his shoulder. Almost lifted her hand to his wild hair, as well, to smooth it out. Her fingers remembered just how soft and clean it felt. For a man whose major concern was the restoration of a princess to the Aragovian throne, he was showing a remarkable attention to the tiniest details of that princess's routine.

He cares.

Despite her lingering anger and mistrust, she kept thinking this. She'd thought it at three o'clock on Wednesday morning, when they tried a pacifier. She'd thought it at seven the next evening, when they tried a warm, soothing bath. She'd thought it when he ordered take-out Chinese that same night before she'd even discovered that she was hungry. And she'd thought it again when he remembered to pick up diapers from the store on Thursday afternoon before she discovered that they'd almost run out.

And she kept stubbornly telling herself that it wasn't enough. It wasn't enough that he cared, when he had a political agenda as well. It wasn't just a question of trust, as he'd said on Sunday. What was he really asking of her? Even more, surely, than what he was asking of Alice. And what was he offering in return?

"Just *out*," Suzanne repeated, her voice rising wildly. "We're getting claustrophobic. We're going nuts and she's picking up on our vibes. Babies are amazing that way. I learned that in the unit, but I've lost it since we came home. She'll relax if we can learn to. I have a key to a community garden on Forty-Eighth Street. It's a mild afternoon. We can bring a picnic blanket and let her lie in the sun, like Terri suggested."

It took them twenty minutes to prepare for such a major expedition. Stephen brushed his hair, which somehow made it look messier than it had before. Suzanne put boiled water in a bottle and packed three diapers, just in case. On the sidewalk at the front of the building, they spent a frantic five minutes working out how to unfold the brand-new stroller and lock it into position. Then they walked the two blocks to the community garden, only stopping three times to adjust the stroller canopy, retuck Alice's blankets and watch her smiling in her sleep.

We're like a family, Suzanne thought, and when they reached the park and settled themselves on the grass, the people who came up to coo over the baby acted as if they were a family, too.

"She has your forehead," a young woman said to Stephen.

"Your eyes," a busy mother told Suzanne a little later, when Alice was awake.

And each resemblance was possible, since Alice was related by blood to both of them.

They stayed in the garden for nearly two hours, until afternoon shadows began to creep across and the deceptive daytime warmth of early fall began to fade. They hardly talked, and when they did, it was always about Alice.

"Do you think there's too much breeze on her face?"

"Look, she's taken three ounces from her bottle!"

"She's falling asleep again. I think the fresh air is tiring her out."

Suzanne wouldn't have felt safe with any other subject. Maybe Stephen wouldn't have, either. Like this, without talking, it was nice. Just as this small, fenced garden gave the illusion of country innocence and freshness in the middle of the huge city, so did their silence give the illusion that they had nothing left to battle over.

The temporary peace between them made Suzanne feel far happier than it should, and that night, asleep on her sofa bed while Alice slumbered in her crib just a few yards away, she dreamed that she was lying in Stephen's arms. She could almost feel the way his mouth wafted warm breath into her hair, the way his hands cupped against her breasts, and she awoke to the sound of Alice's fretting, at two in the morning, with tears in her eyes.

Chapter Eight

Suzanne was sitting at Pixie's wrought-iron table several days later, feeding Alice on her lap, when she heard footsteps just outside the door, and the click of a key in the lock. Stephen, of course.

She met his entrance with a scowl, furious with herself—and him—because she hadn't known where he was all day, it was now after four in the afternoon and she had been worried. He wore the same expensive dark suit he'd worn for their wedding, but he was already pulling off the suit jacket to hang it on a peg behind the door.

He looked tired and not happy.

"Where were you?" she asked. It came out too much like an accusation.

"You're not working today, are you?" he said. She had started back at the library on Monday morning. "You didn't need me to be here to look after her?"

"No, but—" She stopped.

She was determined to avoid an apology, but at the same time realized that she didn't need to behave this way. Did she have the right to expect an account of his movements, with their marriage in the state that it was? No.

"Should we leave notes for each other in future?" she suggested carefully. "If—oh, I don't know! If the baby got sick, or if Mom decided to spring something on us, we should be able to—"

"I'm sorry," he answered. "Yes, I should have told you. It all took longer than expected. I've been at the bank, and at Rankin's," he said. Suzanne recognized the name of a well-known international auction house. "Negotiating the sale of Princess Elizabeth's jewels."

"Oh, Stephen!"

She knew, without having to ask, how much it meant to him. Even though she sometimes felt that she hated the very name of Aragovia, and would have wished the place out of existence if she could, she had to respond to his stricken face.

"It's good news," he said. He dropped into a chair, loosened his tie, rolled his gray shirtsleeves and reached for an orange from the fruit bowl on the table.

"I'll put some coffee on," she murmured, and set Alice down on one of the wrought-iron chairs in her car carrier. This doubled successfully as a place for the baby to lie when, as now, she was alert and wanted to take part in the conversation.

"We got a good price," Stephen continued. "Didn't have to go to auction. Rankin's had a client who wanted to negotiate a preauction sale and was prepared to pay accordingly. I don't know who it was.

There was an agent acting for the buyer—who should be very pleased with him because he was exhaustively thorough!''

He dug his thumb into the orange, tore off the peel in thick chunks, then began to separate the fruit into sections. Its scent was pungent and sweet in the air. Looking at him, in those rolled sleeves with juice at the corner of his gorgeous mouth, you would never have known he'd just spent several hours dealing with a multimillion-dollar jewelry sale. If Suzanne had expected her insistence on staying in this down-market apartment to throw Stephen off track in any way, he was proving her wrong.

"The agent got your back up?'' she asked him, pressing the pleated paper filter into the coffeemaker.

"Not really,'' he admitted. "He was quite justified in going through the details very carefully. I just didn't want to sell.''

"Then why did you?'' In her heart, she knew the answer already, but wanted to hear it again in his own words. There were so many times when, against her will, she had to respect what drove him.

He didn't disappoint her.

"How could I justify keeping those precious pieces, when their sale will make such a difference to health care in my country? We need a modern hospital. My work as regent won't take all my time, by any means. I'll have an important role in setting it up. The palace is available. Aside from the wing I've been given, there are two hundred and forty rooms of a building that's as solid as a rock going to waste because they're shabby and neglected and have no obvious use—now that the KGB and the Communist Party have no further claim on them.''

''How many rooms in your wing?''

''I'm not sure. Thirty-five or forty, someone told me.''

''Oh. Just a tiny bit bigger than this, then!''

''Yes, but it needs a similar amount of work. I'm only using four of the rooms at the moment, and I haven't counted the others.'' He didn't seem to care. He put another piece of orange in his mouth, looked at baby Alice, who was tracking his movements with her deep-blue eyes, and said very seriously, ''Yummy! You just wait, little girl, till you're ready for things like this!''

Then he gave a sudden grin across at Suzanne, his mouth still glistening with juice and his blue eyes wickedly bright. ''I'm going to enjoy planning a use for them all.''

She couldn't help grinning back. The whole apartment was alive with her awareness of him. ''I expect that would be—yes, that would be fun.''

She could imagine the way he'd walk purposefully from room to room. Maybe he'd measure and take notes, or he'd have a designer with him and they'd talk about ceiling height and traffic flow. There would be books of fabric samples and furniture designs to look through, and, yes, it would definitely be fun. He could have a music room, a gym, a library, guest suites for visiting foreign dignitaries, bedrooms for half a dozen beloved royal children....

She shut off the images with a snap, too disturbed about where they were leading her. He wanted her to feel this way. He wanted her to follow Alice, in the wake of her destiny.

"As for the hospital," he added, "With the money from Princess Elizabeth's jewels as an initial investment, we can start work on a refit, purchase the medical equipment and supplies we need."

"Would Princess Elizabeth have been happy about it?"

"Yes. She would."

"You knew her, then?"

"Very well. She only died thirteen years ago. She was a wonderful, courageous woman."

"You never told me how the jewels came to be here. You said you would."

Alice cooed and flapped her little arms, as if she wanted to hear the story, too. Stephen crushed the final section of orange in his mouth, then went to the sink to rinse his face and hands. He wiped them on a clean hand towel then hung it back on its hook on the wall.

Suzanne stood by the coffeemaker, just a few feet away, trying not to watch him. The coffee was dripping into the glass carafe, adding its rich scent to the sweetness of the orange still filling the air. She watched the dark drips instead of Stephen, and only turned when he was safely seated again.

"If you want to hear it, I'll tell you," he said. "I've had the impression you'd put your hands over your ears if I mentioned Aragovia."

"I didn't just now," she pointed out, then added more honestly, "Mostly I want to. The place seems like a black hole to me, waiting to suck Alice up forever."

"It won't be like that. I've tried to tell you."

"It's like that for you. I'm not talking about paparazzi and royal protocol. Aragovia *owns* you, Stephen."

He didn't answer, and she knew she'd hit on a truth he couldn't deny. There was an odd satisfaction to her accurate hit, followed by immediate regret. Pricking at another person's weaknesses didn't make you stronger yourself.

There was a sudden click and shift in her mind as she thought this.

That's Mom. She pricks at other people's weaknesses, at my weaknesses, all the time, but she's not really strong. In so many ways, she's not strong at all.

"Tell me the story," she prompted Stephen as she poured the coffee. She splashed milk into the two mugs, slid both of them across the table, set out a plate of cookies and sat down.

"It was just before the Russian Revolution," he began.

"In 1917?"

"That's right." He sipped his coffee, then reached for a cookie. "My great-grandfather was out of the country at the time, in Switzerland, and he saw it all coming. He would have sent for my great-grandmother to join him abroad, only she was due to deliver a baby any day. So he returned to Aragovia and arranged for most of the family's possessions to be sent on ahead, in the care of servants."

"That can't have been very safe."

"Only one cartload ever arrived, driven by a very loyal man who deposited it in the Swiss bank vault

Peter Christian had set up in advance. We don't know what happened to the rest of the things. There were paintings, clothing, some furniture, more jewelry. Maybe it was looted, or destroyed in outbreaks of fighting. The revolution took over before Princess Elizabeth had recovered from the birth enough to travel.''

"And the baby?"

"It was a little girl. She died at birth."

"Oh, Elizabeth must have been heartbroken!"

"She kept the baby's photograph her whole life," he said. "My mother has it now. She asked about you on the phone the other day, by the way, when I called her."

"I don't want your mother asking about me. What did you tell her?"

"That you were well, and thrilled with Alice's progress."

"I guess I can't fault that. Finish your story."

"When Princess Elizabeth had recovered, she and Peter Christian talked about trying to flee to the west, but decided against it. They felt that the loss of those cartloads of things was a sign to them. That they should share their fate with the Aragovian people. In those early days, there was a lot of hope."

"I know hardly anything about all this."

"The revolution had taken Russia and Aragovia out of the Great War. The Communist message was so full of promise then. Food and education and health care for all. Since my great-grandparents embraced it, and since they were protected by the peasants who knew them and trusted them, they weren't killed as many Russian and Ukrainian nobles were."

"Still, it can't have been easy."

"You're right. At no point was it easy! Aragovia was soon disillusioned with Communism, but Elizabeth and Peter Christian stayed on, still believing it was their duty, and that there was no choice. They kept the Swiss bank vault a secret, afraid that the Soviet government would appropriate its contents. I don't think my uncle Alex knew about it when he left in 1957. My great-grandmother only told us about it shortly before her death, when there were signs that the Soviet empire was losing its power."

"But why is the jewelry here? You stopped in Switzerland a few weeks ago and brought it over to sell, I suppose. Were there no potential buyers in Europe? And what about the other things? The things in those boxes we haven't unpacked? Why are they here?"

"Because I brought them with me when I came to do my family practice training here ten years ago," he answered. "Back then, like my uncle, I was planning to stay."

"But you didn't stay. You went back as soon as you'd finished your training."

Alice began to fret. Suzanne took a last sip of her coffee then stood and picked the baby up. She held her against her shoulder, swaying from side to side to soothe her without even having to think about the movement. Alice quieted at once.

We're getting better at this, the three of us.

"I couldn't stay," Stephen answered. "Jodie thought I was crazy. I suggested that she should come with me. Aragovia was crying out for good doctors. But she wouldn't consider it—what did she owe to that place? she said—and it broke up our friendship in the end. It broke up another relationship, too, with the woman I was involved with at the time.''

"Because you couldn't stay here.''

"I was needed there more.''

"Aragovia owns you.''

Stephen got up from the table, his movements quick in his impatience.

"Yes," he said. "That's the second time you've said it, and it's true. Is that so terrible, Suzanne? To feel so strongly tied to my heritage and my soil?''

He came around to her and spread a cloth diaper on her shoulder. "Here, she's crying again.''

Suzanne felt the practical touch of his fingers like a caress and hated the fact that he could still have this powerful effect on her. The story he'd just told her, too. Against her will, it drew her understanding.

"Let me get this diaper straight," he murmured, and she gave a silent nod, not trusting herself to speak.

Now that they'd relaxed a little more about Alice, everything she'd felt for him during their brief honeymoon was back, and stronger than ever, pulsing in her body like a current, battling with her other feelings toward him and winning every time.

She couldn't hide it from him, either. She felt her whole body begin to soften like ice cream in the sun. Her lips parted. Her eyes widened and wouldn't look away. Her cheeks flooded with heat and she dipped...swayed...a crucial few inches closer to the magnetic aura of his body.

"Don't stain your pretty top," he said, smoothing

the diaper into place. A finger touched her bare neck, and she felt his breath on her cheek.

She gathered her will. "Don't change the subject!"

"All right. Yes, Aragovia owns me, if you want to phrase it that way. Is it wrong? *Why* is it wrong?"

"Because of what it does to you. Because it makes you ruthless."

But he didn't look ruthless now. He had a tissue in his hand, and he was tilting his head a little as he wiped a smear of creamy formula from Alice's chin. His lips were slightly parted, and the pupils of those shadow-blue eyes were wide and dark, beneath his black lashes. His scar was like a silvery thread pulled tight down his cheek, and she noticed the way it nicked the corner of his mouth. She wanted to press the tiny dent with her finger, and with her mouth.

With her little cheek resting against the soft, gauzy cloth of the diaper on Suzanne's shoulder, Alice was starting to drift off to sleep. Stephen stroked the gossamer-fine sheen of hair on her head with one finger, while his other hand rested against the wall, cutting off Suzanne's path of escape from the table.

"Shall we try putting her down?" he said.

"Wait until she's more deeply asleep."

"Her toes are coming out of her suit." He tucked the five little pink peas back in their stretchy mauve pod and fastened the metal snap that had come undone and allowed the toes to escape.

Suzanne thought that she'd escaped, too—escaped his answer to her accusation. But she was wrong.

"Don't you think your definition of *ruthless* is a bit too loose?" he said, looking up at her suddenly. He was still standing so close that his gray shirtfront brushed Alice's diaper-padded bottom. "Is it ruthless to care about what happens to my people? I care, and I'm prepared to do something about it."

"You're ruthless with me," she repeated stubbornly. Their eyes were locked together, now, green on blue and blue on green. He bent a little closer and her mouth was two inches from his. She could have dropped her head and escaped, but she didn't.

"Then I might as well kiss you and properly earn my terrible reputation," he muttered, and she didn't try to stop him when his lips at last reached her mouth.

The drowsy baby in Suzanne's arms was no protection for her at all. Alice probably liked the feeling of being sandwiched between two warm, gently moving bodies. With both hands free, Stephen had the advantage. He knew it, and he used it deliberately, pinning her by the shoulders and pressing her back until her shoulder blades were hard against the wall.

He tasted of coffee and his mouth was delicious, relentless, wickedly erotic and unashamedly hungry. Suzanne's breathing grew ragged in seconds, and when he took a step to bring his thighs against hers, she rocked her hips forward instinctively to deepen their contact, pressing her breasts against his chest as well.

"I think I like being ruthless," he said, his words a part of their kiss. "I like making you respond, feeling how you share this. If ruthlessness is about strength and passion, Suzanne, if it's about having the ability to see a goal and go after it with everything you have, then you're as ruthless as I am. You were ruthless about our marriage. You wanted it. If I could only make you see that Aragovia isn't the enemy.''

"All right. Aragovia isn't the enemy. You're the enemy," she said.

"I'm not."

"This is, then. What you can make me feel."

"I can still make you feel it, can't I, even though you're angry and stubborn and full of fight?''

"Yes. And I'm going to hate you for it, soon."

"You don't mean that. Put Alice down and come to bed. Maybe you'll see it differently if we make love again. I want to touch you, and hear your cries. That was real, Suzanne, you know it was."

"Yes. For me it was. Real and precious, and you bruised it so badly afterward. So badly, Stephen!" Her lower lip trembled.

"Without meaning to." His mouth whispered against hers once more, nipping that lower lip in a soft bite, lapping his tongue against hers. His hands ran down her back, pulled her hips still closer, then slid toward her breasts, cupping and lifting their weight, teasing her nipples. "It was just as real and precious to me. I couldn't pretend or lie about something like that."

"No? You managed to lie pretty well about other things!"

The words Suzanne had just spoken brought her to her senses. Snap! It was like a sudden jolt of whiplash on a roller coaster. She twisted her face to the side, making one shoulder blade press painfully against the wall.

"Move," she said. "Stop this. You're trapping me."

"If you want." He stepped back, but took her hand at once, as if he were somehow compelled to maintain their body contact. His fingers tangled with hers, stroking the thin skin on the back of her hand, sliding into the sensitive hollows between each finger. He closed thumb and forefinger around her wrist like a bracelet, then simply clasped her hand, palm against palm, and didn't move.

"You couldn't resist, could you?" she said, her other arm shaking as she held the sleeping baby close to her. The sweet, milky scent of Alice's feather-light breath wafted to her nose. "Couldn't resist proving to me that I still wanted this."

"It *was* real!" he insisted. "It still is, and I don't think it's going to go away."

"Yes, and isn't that convenient for you?" She twisted out of his grip. "It doesn't *change* anything, Stephen! That's what you don't understand. This attraction doesn't change anything. Jodie wouldn't sacrifice her life to Aragovia. You told me that just now. Why should Jodie's daughter do it?"

"Because things are different there, now. And because it's right. Necessary. That doesn't mean it's easy. The right thing isn't always the easy thing, Suzanne. At this very moment, the right thing seems like the hardest thing in the world, to me."

"Then *prove* to me that it's right! Prove to me that I should listen to your vision of things. Don't prove that you can get me into bed."

"No? That's something I'd like to prove, very much."

"You've proved it already. You can get me into bed, Stephen! Believe that. It's not in doubt. I'm—"

she took a breath "—melting for you. Hot for you. I hadn't known it could be like this. That I could want a man like this. I never have, like this, before. Don't make me hate you for it. Don't use it."

"I wouldn't. I haven't."

"No? Move!" she repeated, because he hadn't. Hadn't even let go of her hand. He could feel exactly how hot and shaky it was. "I'm going to put Alice down, now," she said. "Then I'm going out. I've been stuck in this apartment all day with a fussy baby who apparently belongs to Aragovia, not to me, and I'm going *out!*"

Suzanne walked for an hour.

The streets were crowded with homeward-bound commuters, and darkness was coming on. Not caring where she went, she found herself at the community garden where they had taken Alice last week, but the place looked chilly, deserted and unfriendly at this hour and in any case she needed to walk, not sit.

Reaching Fifth Avenue, she wandered past the lit up windows of expensive stores and couldn't help lingering at the jewelry displays. She saw nothing that compared to Princess Elizabeth's tiara and necklace, and wondered who would next wear those lovely things. Would their new owner appreciate the richness of their history, and the depth of Stephen's sacrifice in selling them?

Suzanne couldn't imagine so.

When she arrived back at the apartment, Alice was still asleep and she could smell hot food. Stephen had gotten pizza delivered, and he'd made some salad as well. She saw the bowl of dressed greens in the middle of the table, and the pizza box balanced near the sink.

It was the table that fully caught her attention, however. It was set with a clean but slightly yellowed damask cloth, napkins and napkin rings, polished silverware, gold-rimmed plates and candlesticks.

"What's this?" she demanded.

"To show you. A surprise, I suppose. I thought you would be interested. I opened those boxes belonging to my great-grandparents, just now. Here's the Serkin-Rimsky crest on the china and silverware, see? There are photo albums and other things, but we'll look at those later."

"I'd like to." But she was wary, all the same. She picked up a solid silver napkin ring and traced the embossed heraldic crest and motto. *"Bien servir le patrimoine,"* she read aloud. "Is that Aragovian?"

"French. About 250 years ago, the ruling prince married a French noblewoman and she translated our family motto into French. She felt Aragovian wasn't a sufficiently elevated language."

"What does it mean?"

"To serve the heritage well. It's hard to translate with the elegance of the original."

He pulled out a chair for her and she sat, hardly noticing either his movement or hers. The table setting had mesmerized her. The plates were beautiful and simple, just plain cream china with a thin gold rim and crest. She turned one over and found the name of a famous English china company.

"This set is over a hundred years old," Stephen told her.

"And we're having take-out pizza on it?"

"I like that." He grinned as he put the box on the table, opened it up and offered her a slice on a silver cake trowel. "Pizza, Madame la Princesse?"

"Why thank you, Your Highness…. Stephen, I know what you're doing! Or what you're *trying* to do!"

He poured soda into a crystal wineglass. "That's because I'm not being very subtle about it."

"Would there be any way to exercise subtlety in this situation?"

"I couldn't think of one, so I decided not to try. Yes, I'm hoping to show you what Alice's heritage has to offer her."

"She would grow up eating from these plates."

"When she wasn't using her set featuring her favorite cartoon characters. At five years old, or nine, or twelve, being a princess is by no means a full-time job."

"She'd have to learn the correct etiquette for state dinners."

"Her ancestors wouldn't just be a series of names on a family tree. They'd mean something to her. There are other things in the boxes, too, Suzanne. More personal things. Princess Elizabeth's wedding dress and veil. A silver baby's rattle and a christening gown. A piece of embroidery done by Peter Christian's mother when she was a child, with some crooked stitches in it and an ink stain on the hem. The people in my family lived and suffered, laughed and learned like anyone else."

"After we've eaten, I'll let you show me the photo albums."

"Shall we light these candles?"

"I think the silverware might start a whispering campaign against us if we don't. I'm sure these knives and forks consider it their birthright to gleam beneath candlelight, not a fluorescent tube."

He laughed. "I think you could be right." He found a box of matches on top of the fridge and lit two candles, each set in a silver candlestick. Suzanne watched the movement of his hands, and the way his blue eyes focused on what he was doing.

"Are we the first people to eat from these plates since 1917?" she asked.

"I washed them, I promise." He sat down again and smiled at her.

"I didn't mean—"

"I know you didn't."

He held his glass up to hers and they clinked them together. "Yes, we are the first. I like that. It's the way it should be, don't you think?"

Suzanne could hardly eat, and couldn't talk at all. Stephen seemed comfortable with their silence, maybe even pleased about it. He had disarmed her, pulled the rug from under her feet by openly admitting to what he was doing with this scene of staged elegance. For a man who had been so happy to manipulate her feelings in the beginning, he was now showing a much greater openness than she might once have thought him capable of.

But I've changed, too.

The knowledge frightened her for two reasons. First, that little word *too*. Had he really changed as a person, or had he just changed his tactics? Second, her own sense of being different. She was more aware of her own strength, more confident about her perceptions. And at times she'd started to almost enjoy their battles.

Most of all, she understood the full depth of her attraction to Stephen and was more comfortable about it than she could have imagined two weeks ago. They were both adults. She could feel this way about him without shame. She could let it show in her face and know she was giving nothing away. It was already out in the open, as apparent to their senses as incense in the air, or music, or the taste of chocolate. How much did it mean?

After the meal, they looked at mementos and photo albums for an hour, since Alice still slept, and Suzanne was left with a tangle of vivid impressions. The christening gown and wedding dress were both made of French lace. The silver rattle was musical and heavy. It still seemed impossible that Alice would one day have the strength to shake it and produce a sound.

The albums showed a thick-walled palace of gray stone like a fairy-tale castle, set against the backdrop of forested mountain slopes. There were formal gardens and landscaped meadows running down to a lake, and stone houses tightly clustered into a substantial and picturesque town.

Most of the photos were more personal than this, though. She saw bearded men in thick, old-fashioned clothing, fishing in a stream or posed with the game they had shot. She saw women in long dark skirts, laughing as they attempted a primitive form of skiing. There were posed family portraits, and some official pictures, too, showing serious, statesmanlike figures shaking hands.

And there were baby pictures.

"That's my grandfather, Albert," Stephen said. "He was born in 1913."

"But he looks so much like Alice. You knew I'd see it straight away, didn't you?"

"Should I have taken those photos out of the album?"

"No, I guess not."

"Don't assume that everything is part of a strategy, Suzanne."

"Perhaps you could let me know which things are, and which aren't."

"I'm trying to, now."

He looked at her steadily, and all of a sudden her sense of strength came crashing down around her. She felt like a fish on the end of a line. Just because she was fighting him with everything she had, that didn't mean she had the slightest chance of winning.

Chapter Nine

Stephen couldn't get to sleep.

He thought he had resigned himself to the broken pattern of his nights, but this was different. Alice had gone to sleep again after a fussy two hours, and almost immediately Suzanne retreated to her screened-off bed. Feeling majorly sleep deprived himself, he knew there was no point in staying up. He didn't want to disturb Suzanne or Alice with the sound of the TV, and that was about all he had the energy for.

He went to the kitchen end of the apartment for a glass of water, and could hear her undressing just a few yards away. Didn't think he'd ever heard such a seductive series of sounds. There were two soft thuds as she set her clunky shoes on the floor, and a swish as she slid her skirt down her thighs.

A little later, he heard the unmistakable click of a bra clip unfastening. His stomach muscles tensed at the picture the sound evoked. Blood rushed from his extremities to converge at his core. Then came the rumple of moving fabric and the squeak of metal springs as she climbed into bed. His discomfort climbed several notches.

Yet he was used to this lack of privacy. Having grown up in a two-room apartment, he knew these sounds by heart. They shouldn't disturb him like this.

Once he was in bed himself, his imagination continued to torture him. During their broken nights this past week, he'd seen the nightdress she wore and it was perfect for her—a fine, flowing garment of dainty white cotton fabric. He could picture how it would look on her, its folds whispering against her skin and becoming almost transparent when Alice's night-light was behind her. Suzanne herself probably considered it a chaste thing, and had no idea of its seductive power.

What would happen if he simply threw back his covers, stepped around these pretty, foolish screens and took Suzanne in his arms? He'd dispose of the white cotton in seconds. It would make no barrier at all against his hands. How many different ways would there be to take it off, or tear it, perhaps, rip it from neck to hem and feel her breasts spilling into his hands…?

Stop, stop!

Back at the kitchen sink, he drank a second glass of water then splashed more water, cold and fresh, onto his face. It did no good at all. In the end he just lay there, listening for the baby's first cry as the hours passed. He was handling Alice's night wakings between two and six, so that Suzanne could have at least one unbroken stretch of rest.

They were both tired. Maybe that was why he felt so angry with her, suddenly. He knew it wasn't her fault, but that somehow didn't help.

This is not what I expected or wanted when I came to America. I didn't want to learn to see the question of Alice's future from Suzanne's point of view. I didn't want to care about how she feels, want her this badly, or understand so vividly what she's afraid of.

There had to be a way to make sure that Alice had the things Suzanne wanted for her. He knew what they were, at least. Love and simplicity and the chance to grow in her own way.

But maybe Suzanne was right. Maybe he couldn't promise those things when what he also wanted, just as strongly, was for Alice to serve Aragovia. Just as it said on the crest on the china and silverware. *Bien servir le patrimoine.* To serve the heritage well.

He wanted that for her, and Suzanne wanted other things, and he didn't know how they would ever get it to mesh together. And he was angry. With her. With himself. Because he didn't want it to be like this!

Meanwhile, the hearing on the issue of permanent custody for Alice was scheduled to take place next week.

"I'm taking her for a little walk, that's all," Rose said to Suzanne. "We won't talk to strangers, will we, boodyful? We won't give you candy, or any bad fings for little Alice's tum-tum, will we, angel-love?"

"Not even too much bottle all at once, Mom, because it'll come right back up. And not more than an hour and a half, because then she has to go back on her oxygen mask."

"Honey, you've told me all this. A mother never forgets, okay? Doctors are too stuck on numbers, don't you think? She's not on the oxygen now, and she looks fine."

"Mom...!"

"I'll have her back for the oxygen. Of course I will. An hour and a half. Maybe I'll buy her an outfit, or something." Rose seemed as excited as a child about the outing with her tiny granddaughter.

"The pediatrician said she isn't to be indoors with crowds of people," Suzanne warned, feeling as if she were bursting a little girl's balloon.

"Oh, okay, no shopping," Rose agreed at once, sounding slightly breathless. "Honey, relax! How much weight did the pediatrician say she'd put on in the last week?"

"Three and a half ounces."

"See! She's thriving. She looks like a regular baby, now."

Suzanne helped Rose carry baby and stroller and diaper bag down the stairs, squashed down her nerves as she waved them goodbye, then returned to the apartment and tried to do something useful. A nap? No, she knew she wouldn't sleep. The dishes? Done in five minutes. Laundry, then. There was plenty of it now that she had Alice home.

Dressed casually in jeans, athletic shoes and a blue stretchy top, she put together a bag of things to take down to the laundromat. She left a note on the door to say where she was and when she'd be back, in case Rose and Alice returned before she was done. The lock on the building's front door was broken at the moment, so they'd be able to get inside.

The note was for Stephen, too. He'd had a phone call from Arkady Radouleau this morning, and had gone to meet him somewhere. Apparently he hadn't known what it was going to be about.

The Ninth Avenue laundromat was noisy and too warm. Breathing air that was thick and heavy with lint and acrid with the smell of scented detergents, Suzanne waited out her wash cycle with the circle and drop, circle and drop of someone else's dryer load blurring in front of her. The tangle of the clothing had too much in common with the tangle of her mind.

It was likely that next week's meeting with Dr. Feldman and the family court representative would provide some answers, but it wasn't certain. If Feldman's decision went in favor of Rose, Suzanne didn't know if she'd be able to accept it. Would she challenge his recommendation and take it all the way to a formal court proceeding?

There were cases like this which had gone on for years. Conflicting parties fought over a child like a pair of three-year-olds fighting over a doll. The image was too vivid in her mind. Sometimes, dolls got broken in those fights.

I couldn't do it to Alice, she knew. *I couldn't risk damaging her by creating such a cloud of uncertainty over her life. I'd let Mom win rather than do that, and hope that her victory would keep her sweet, that she'd let me stay in Alice's life. She's promised that she would, but I hold my breath over Mom's promises at the best of times.*

Would Stephen accept a verdict in favor of Rose, though? No. He would take the whole matter to the arena of international affairs if he had to, for Aragovia's sake.

And maybe that was the only real issue now. Maybe neither she nor Rose actually counted at all. There seemed to be no room for compromise in what Stephen wanted. Even when Suzanne had come closer to understanding his viewpoint, she'd never seen a chink of space left over inside him for compromise.

Loading her laundry into the dryer, she put it on low heat to protect Alice's delicate baby things, then was too impatient and churned up so she wouldn't have to wait the extra time it took them to dry, and bundled everything back into her laundry bag after twenty minutes, when it was still slightly damp.

She thought Rose would be back with Alice. She was due to go back on the oxygen mask soon. It was important, because she still couldn't quite keep her blood oxygen level up to normal on room air alone. The pediatrician had her up to an hour and a half break, now, but this weaning from the mask had to be gradual as her strength and lung capacity increased.

But when Suzanne reached her building, its corridors were quiet, and Rose and the baby weren't waiting out front or at the top of the stairs. The note on the door was undisturbed. She looked at her watch. Alice had been off her mask for an hour and thirty-five minutes.

The footsteps she was listening for out in the corridor came five minutes later, while she was still hanging the damp laundry over crib rails and chair backs. Her hands were getting shaky with fear, and her palms were a lot wetter than the little stretchy suits. She dropped a garment into the crib and ran to the door.

"Mom! Thank goodness! You've been gone too—" But she broke off as she got the door open, because it wasn't Mom, it was Stephen, just about to push his key into the lock. "Oh!"

She stepped back, her disappointment coming as a sudden wave of nausea. She'd told Mom an hour and a half.

"You were expecting Rose?" he said. He was wearing his suit, the expensive dark garment that made him look so formidable, so successful and so much like a winner. He had a briefcase in his hand and a glow in his face that she didn't have the time or the focus to identify right now.

"Yes." She turned on her heel, unable to face him, unable to deal with the way he tore her apart. Heaven help her, she could have loved him so easily in other circumstances. Her body knew it. Her heart knew it.

"What's wrong?" he demanded. "You've gone white."

"Mom took Alice for a walk," she said. "An hour and forty minutes ago."

"But she has to go on the oxygen again after—"

"I know. I mean, it's not critical. Not yet. But Mom has to get back soon."

"Why did you let them go?" He stepped into the apartment, closed the door and flung his briefcase onto the kitchen table.

"We have the meeting with Feldman next week." She spread her hands. "I wanted to keep her sweet. Whether he decides in favor of us or Mom and Perry, I can't afford to have her hostile. Either she'll for-

mally contest Feldman's decision, or she wouldn't let
me see the baby. I—I'm terrified about both of those
things.''

"And is that the only reason, Suzanne? Keeping
her sweet?'' he said gently.

She looked at him. ''No. No, it's not.'' She sighed.
''It's because she's my mother. But that doesn't mean
I trust her.''

She pressed her hands to her face and felt dry sobs
shaking her shoulders. He cradled her against his
chest. ''Shh...it's all right. They'll be back soon.''

But another hour passed, and there was no sign of
Rose. It was almost four-thirty now, and the deceptive
afternoon warmth had drained from the October day.

''Why did I let her go? I should never have let
them go....''

''Should we call her hotel?''

''Don't you think I would have done it already? I
don't know where they're staying now. She just said
'something cheaper.' Almost every hotel in New
York is cheaper than where they were staying before.''

''Their home number in Philly? They would have
had time to drive there by now.''

''What's the point, Stephen? If Mom has...taken
her deliberately, kidnapped her—'' she could hardly
say it ''—that's the last place she'd go.'' Her mouth
was as dry as chalk.

''Give me the number,'' he said. ''I'm going to try
anyway. Maybe Perry's there. There's probably a perfectly reasonable explanation.''

Stephen went to the phone, but his silence, after a
long wait, told her he was getting no reply. He cut

the connection, and immediately keyed in three more numbers.

"What are you doing now?"

"Calling 911."

"We're doing everything we can to find the baby, Mrs. Serkin-Rimsky," the police detective said.

His use of her new married name added to the jarring sense of unreality that had taken possession of Suzanne over the past five hours. Every minute that had passed and every step the police had taken confirmed that there wasn't a harmless explanation for Rose's disappearance with Alice.

They were treating it as a definite kidnapping case, now.

They'd tracked down Rose's hotel. She and Perry hadn't checked out, but neither of them were on the premises. They'd checked hospitals and accident reports, but no one answering Rose's description had been brought in, with or without a baby. Now they'd started checking transport out of the city, and were asking more questions.

Who were Rose's main contacts? What was her bank balance? Did she ever use any other name? What make and model of car did Perry drive?

"Dr. Feldman," the detective said now, "how critical is the baby's need for breathing assistance?"

The pediatrician had been here at the apartment since six, coming straight from his practice after Suzanne had called him there.

"It's hard to say." His mouth was pursed with stress, and his balding forehead sheened with sweat. "I've talked to the baby's own doctor and he can't

give a precise opinion, either. It depends on how well
Rose is caring for her, and how long before we can
track them down.''

"Mom would never harm her deliberately," Suzanne interjected. "This is some weird idea of hers
about the custody issue. She's caring for Alice, I
know she is.''

"But she may not have your vigilance, Suzanne,"
Dr. Feldman replied, his voice slurred with reluctance. "And she doesn't have Alice's apnea alarm
with her. That's my greatest concern.''

Suzanne went cold, then felt Stephen's arms fold
around her as he cradled her from behind. He pressed
his mouth against her hair and her neck, supported
her weakened limbs with his own strength. He didn't
try to comfort her with words, because they both
knew there were no words for this.

"Suzanne, I'm so sorry," Dr. Feldman said. "I
blame myself for all of this.''

"No," she answered thinly. "You mustn't.''

He looked as if he were about to argue, then simply
shook his head, seeming a lot older than his fifty-three
years.

There was another stretched out and painful inter-
lude of nerve-jangling questions and police activity.
Suzanne served coffee and cookies for everyone as if
running on a computer program, but couldn't take a
mouthful of supper herself. Finally, they'd all gone.
Dr. Feldman had wanted to stay, but Suzanne had
practically pushed him out the door to go home and
get some rest. He'd looked ill with strain and fatigue.
Now she was alone with Stephen.

"We'll be on this all night," the detective had told

them as he left. "We'll call as soon as there's any news."

"Do you want to try to sleep, Suzanne?" Stephen asked.

"No."

"Michael gave me something for you. It's an over-the-counter pill. It's not strong, but it would help."

"I can't bear this...."

"I know. I know."

They held each other.

"Where is she? If Mom sleeps... Mom *must not* sleep! There's no alarm to waken her if Alice stops breathing, and she's been off the oxygen for nine hours, now...."

"Don't. Don't, my darling." He kissed her. Kissed her closed lids, wild hair, fear-numbed mouth, tear-drenched lashes.

"Stephen..."

"I won't let you go. I'll never let you go, Suzanne."

"Help me. Talk to me. Make love to me." She took his face in her hands and forced his mouth open with her kisses.

"Not now. Not now, darling." His mouth brushed hers gently, taking the thinnest edge off her desperation.

"I'm sorry." She shuddered.

"It's all right." His hands ran down her back. "Take the pill Michael left for you. He was very concerned for your health and you need to rest. When Alice is safely back—"

"Oh!" His words felt like a knife in her heart, as

if the hope in them wasn't safe to speak aloud. "No, I can't afford to sleep."

"You've kept vigil over Alice for three months and more, Suzanne. It's my turn, now. Let yourself sleep," he begged her. "Sleep in my arms and I'll wait for news of her all night."

"If you weren't here, I don't know how I'd—"

"Shh! I'm here. I'll always be here."

Once more, their lips met and crushed hotly together.

"I love you."

"I love you."

"I love you."

Suzanne didn't know who had said it first, who had echoed it, who had repeated it. It didn't matter. It was true for both of them, the only thing that made any sense, the only thing safe enough to cling to, and it existed beyond conflict and duty, beyond fear, beyond the future.

"I love you...." He whispered it again, kissed her again. "Now sleep, darling. Sleep!"

Eventually, she did, fully dressed in her stretch jeans and athletic shoes and periwinkle-blue top, pillowed against his chest on the silver-gray couch.

Stephen paced the darkened apartment, with a mug of strong coffee warming the palms of his hands.

It was almost three in the morning. He'd eased himself out from beneath Suzanne's warm, sleeping body two hours ago, but she hadn't stirred. Carefully, he'd stretched her out into a more comfortable position, removed her shoes and covered her in the blue-and-white striped comforter from her bed. It had slipped a little now, so he straightened it and began to pace once more.

Arriving at the windows that faced the street, he watched the activity across at the cab repair garage. Its lights were the main source of illumination in the room, and he could hear some machine screaming. Thoughts swam through his head as idle and directionless as fish in a bowl, before locking into a painful and familiar track.

What will it do to Suzanne if we lose Alice? I'll spend as long as it takes helping her to heal. Dear God, I don't know what's going to happen, but this love we've found so fast is the center of the universe for me now, and I'm not going to lose it. I'm not going to lose Suzanne.

He gulped some coffee and paced again, his eyes dry and stinging from lack of sleep, and his shoulders aching with tension. When the downstairs buzzer sounded, it took him three seconds to realize what it was, and another four seconds to reach the intercom beside the door.

He heard a male voice that he didn't recognize, and shouted, "Yes, yes, I'll buzz you in!" without even trying to understand what the man was saying. Into his mind floated another aimless fish of a thought. *Maintenance has fixed that front door....*

His shouting had woken Suzanne, of course. She came stiffly toward him, eyelids creased, voice creaky. "Is it the police?"

"I don't know."

"If it's the police... Dear God, if it's the police..."

He saw the dread in her face. "Yes, I know," he answered, and his stomach rolled.

They'd have called if it was good news. Bad news was delivered in person.

She was gasping, her sobs high and jerky in her chest. "Suzanne, Suzanne." He held her again, saying her name over and over, and they both listened, paralyzed, to the heavy male feet coming up the stairs.

He got to the door just before the footsteps did, and dragged it open.

Perry stood there, with Alice in his arms. "I expect you've been worried," he said.

She was blue around the mouth, but she was alive. Oh, thanks be to God, she was alive! Suzanne took the feather-light sleeping baby from Perry at once, sobs still racking her body. Sobs of relief, now.

She took Alice straight to her little screened-off bedroom, where the oxygen tank and mask and breathing alarm were still set up, laid her in her crib, attached the mask to her face and adjusted the oxygen flow to the level Alice had needed several weeks ago. She had to will her hands not to waste time with their shaking.

Behind her, Stephen was questioning Perry. "Where's Rose?"

"At my sister June's house in Springfield."

"*Where?*"

"Massachusetts. Rose called me at seven from a motel in Waterbury. She'd rented a car and an infant seat."

"The police checked the car rental companies. Rose Wigan and Rose Brown."

"She still has a valid credit card in the name of

Chaloner.'' He resumed his story. ''She wanted me to meet her at the motel—''

''Why there?''

''No reason. She…wasn't thinking very clearly. It wasn't a kidnapping attempt. She'd been obsessing over the idea she wasn't getting a fair chance to prove herself. She just wanted to show Feldman that she could take care of Alice as well as anyone else. She was planning to return the baby in a couple of days, healthy and thriving, with a big 'I told you so.' It was a crazy plan. She's—'' his well-bred Boston drawl suddenly cracked ''—obviously not well. Emotionally.''

''A breakdown?''

''It's been building for days. Maybe longer. I'm—worried about her.'' The colorless words didn't disguise his depth of feeling.

He really loves her, Suzanne realized.

''Come in,'' Stephen said. ''You need coffee, I think.''

Perry nodded wearily and kept talking. ''It took me a while to persuade her to give up the idea, and she wouldn't let me call anyone, flushed Suzanne's phone number down the motel toilet. My sister is looking after her. I drove her up there. I couldn't think of what to do.''

He took the coffee Stephen held out to him and drank two deep gulps.

''The baby stopped breathing once at the motel,'' he continued. ''And then four times in the car, as I got close to the city. It was getting more frequent. Her breathing muscles were growing tired without the oxygen, or something. I was terrified. I could see she was starting to look blue around the mouth.''

"Why didn't you take her to a hospital?" Stephen asked.

"They'd have asked questions. I thought we'd lose any chance of having this sorted out without Rose being charged for kidnapping.''

"We won't be pressing charges, Perry," Suzanne said, then looked at Stephen and saw his tiny nod. "Not when she's had a breakdown.''

Perry nodded, couldn't seem to speak.

"What did you do to get her breathing again?" she asked.

She stood beside Alice's crib, not yet daring to leave the baby for a moment. She would call Dr. Feldman soon, get him to come over and check Alice out, although she seemed fine. She was breathing, sleeping. Her eyelids were flickering. Her mouth was pink again, now, through the transparent, familiar mask. Something wonderful suddenly happened in her baby dream, and she smiled.

"I stroked her chest," Perry answered. "It didn't take much to get her started again.''

"No, it never does," Suzanne said. "I tickle her feet." She laughed, with tears still streaming down her cheeks.

"But I had to make sure I noticed when she stopped. That was the hard part. I had to have her beside me in the front seat, with her carrier facing backward. I watched her more than I watched the road. Oh, dear Lord…'' His neat shoulders shook for a moment.

"Perry, it's okay." Impulsively, she crossed the room and kissed his cheek.

He froze. He smiled. Then he said, "You think I went after your mother because I assumed she had money, don't you?"

"I'm sorry, I shouldn't have made an assumption like—"

"I did, of course." He smiled again, crookedly. "Plastic surgery clinics make fertile hunting ground. But then something happened. I fell in love with her. We're two of a kind, Rose and I."

"Is that how it is?"

"And how it's going to stay. I'm sure it's a relief to both of you to know that we won't be pursuing our custody claim."

"Oh, Perry, yes!" Suzanne said.

"Is she all right?" Stephen asked a little later, coming to stand beside Suzanne, who was still leaning on the top rail of Alice's crib, watching her.

Dr. Feldman would be here soon to check the baby's condition, and Stephen had called the police as well, to tell them the news. In Suzanne's bed, Perry snored. For the first time in their difficult acquaintance, Suzanne actually believed he was really asleep.

"She seems fine," she answered Stephen. "Look at her!" Alice was stirring, stretching, arching her little back, pressing her arms out and scrunching her fists and toes. "She's waking up."

"That doesn't give us much time."

"Why do we need time?"

He took her in his arms. "This is how we first met, do you remember? Watching Alice sleep."

"I remember," she answered softly. "It's not that long ago."

"And from the beginning, we felt something. It's grown so fast. We said it to each other tonight, when we clung together in so much pain. I love you, Suzanne. How can we make it work? I don't have an answer. All I can promise you is that I'll do anything to find one."

Suzanne looked up into his eyes, which were dark and shadowed in the dim light. Instinctively, she reached up to smooth away his troubled frown with her fingers, then let them drift to his mouth to trace the line of his lips, pausing at the tiny dent in one corner. He caught her hand in his, kissed her palm, her knuckles, her wrist.

And suddenly it was simple.

"We'll go to Aragovia, the three of us, together, as soon as the doctor says Alice is strong and well enough to travel," she said.

But he shook his head. "You never wanted that. For yourself or for Alice. You've fought that all the way. I'm not prepared to ask for a sacrifice like that from you, Suzanne. Not anymore."

"It's not a sacrifice when we love each other," she answered. "Love makes it different, Stephen."

"How?"

"It makes *everything* different. I didn't want to go on sufferance as Alice's mother substitute and your political wife. I didn't want you to take me only because I was a necessary part of the package. I didn't want Alice to grow up with one parent who only cared about her role as a princess, and another who was resentful and unhappy and unsure of her place."

"I will never let you be unhappy."

"I know that now. You've shown me tonight. I couldn't let myself love you when all you could think about was duty and destiny and that family motto of yours which I can't pronounce. But tonight, when Alice was gone and we were afraid for her life and the only thing we could cling to was each other... Were you thinking of Aragovia then?"

She already knew the answer to the question.

"Not for a moment." His mouth brushed hers.

"I knew it," she whispered.

"Not for a moment, and I can prove it." He laughed suddenly, with a joy she'd never seen in him before. "I can *prove* it, Suzanne!"

He let her go so abruptly that she almost tripped over her own socked feet. "Stop, Stephen!" she said, following him. She was laughing now, too. "I believe you! You don't have to prove anything to me now."

Ignoring her, he went to the kitchen table, where his briefcase still sat, untouched since he'd dropped it there twelve hours ago. He snapped it open, and fiddled inside. She heard two resonant clicks, then saw the flash of something—something pale that moved and flowed in his hands like water in moonlight.

It was Princess Elizabeth's necklace. He threaded it around her throat, above the rounded neckline of her blue top. "Stephen, I don't understand," she said.

"When I came home...home to you and Alice...this afternoon, I could hardly wait to tell you. But as soon as I saw your white, frightened face, I forgot that this briefcase even existed. Arkady Radouleau was the mystery buyer of the necklace and tiara. He has given them to the Aragovian nation for permanent museum display and use by the royal family on state occasions. Will you wear them for me, Suzanne?''

He fastened the clasp, slid it to the nape of her neck and made a trail of kisses that followed the lacy curve of diamonds and gold.

"Now?"

He held her and looked down into her eyes. "Now, and when we renew our marriage vows in Saint Catherine's Cathedral?''

"Yes, oh yes, Stephen, I will.''

Epilogue

It was New Year's Day. From the cathedral in the center of Braudeburg, Aragovia's capital, bells tolled and pealed in the clear air. The Voltzin Mountains, forming a backdrop to the city, were sparkling in a blanket of pristine new snow. Fine, glinting crystals frosted the slate-tile roofs of the capital so that the old stone houses looked like wedding cakes or gingerbread. Christmas colors filled the streets, tiny lights garlanded the bare trees and the whole place was prepared for celebration.

Aragovia's new parliament had sat for its first session this morning, to ratify the new constitution and formally invite Stephen to act as Alice's regent until she was of an age to reign. Now, it seemed as if half the population of the country had lined the route from palace to cathedral, waiting for their chance to cheer for the baby princess and her royal guardians, who were soon to make a ceremonial renewal of their wedding vows.

Wearing her locally made wedding dress of specially woven cream silk, and Princess Elizabeth's gorgeous necklace and tiara, Suzanne stood at the window of her freshly renovated palace suite, with a prayer on her lips.

"Let me live up to all this. This past month since we came here has been so extraordinary. Let me make Stephen the right wife, now and always."

Her frown caught the attention of her sisters, dressed in the matching forest-green silk gowns they were wearing as matrons of honor. They had arrived from America only this morning, as various commitments on Gray McCall's ranch and in Patrick Callahan's software company had made it difficult to get away for long.

As Suzanne had been present, with Alice and Stephen, at the opening of parliament until noon, she'd hardly seen her sisters or the others, and at the state luncheon there had been no opportunity for private conversation. Now Jill's soft, loving arms came around her, and Cat was standing close as well.

There was a knock at the heavy oak door and it swung open. *"Milaya,* are you ready?"

"Oh, Natalya, am I late?"

Suzanne hurried forward to meet Stephen's mother, who was still a little frail following her extensive cancer surgery several months ago, but getting stronger each day. Suzanne was familiar, now, with the Russian endearment Natalya had used.

"A little late," Natalya answered. "You are supposed to be! But now it's time. Stephen and Arkady will be waiting at the cathedral." She kissed Suzanne warmly. "And I'm taking Alice for you, but I haven't seen her in her pretty dress, yet."

"She's here. She's awake and ready."

"Oh, my baby love!" Natalya Serkin-Rimsky cooed and clucked as she caught sight of the baby, who was lying on a padded quilt on the floor, wearing a dress of silk taffeta in her grandmother's favorite pink and batting at her baby gym with eager little hands.

Alice had kicked off her pink booties, and Suzanne had to smile secretly when she heard Natalya say, as she picked them up, "I don't think you need these anymore, my precious."

I don't need little pink booties anymore, either.

Now six months old, Princess Alice had become a supremely good-natured baby. She went happily into her adoptive grandmother's arms, and Natalya hugged her close. "Isn't it lucky I've brought you some brand-new satin slippers to match your dress, my love!" she crooned.

"Are there many photographers, Natalya, do you know?" Suzanne asked nervously.

"Yes, and reporters, and cannons for a salute, and security guards, and concealed marksmen, but they are all keeping to their places," Natalya said. "We can pretend they're not there, and they'll soon go away."

Suzanne laughed. "I'm telling myself that. Not sure if it's helping." She knew that Cat and Jill were both watching her anxiously.

"My dear," Natalya said, "We used to have KGB and gangsters and soldiers. Don't fret about a few cameras, or about people with guns when they are on *our* side! They are not important. Get it all in perspective, Suzanne.''

''You're right.'' She had begun to learn this and so much more about the life that lay ahead of her and Alice, since winding up her life in America and coming to this place a month ago.

She and Stephen had consulted with designers together over the restoration of their thirty-eight rooms in the palace, which was well underway. The conversion of the remaining wings into Stephen's dreamed-of hospital would soon begin. Aragovia was more beautiful than she'd dared to imagine, and Stephen's mother was a jewel more precious than any of the ones in Princess Elizabeth's necklace.

Today everything Stephen had hoped for was coming together, and Suzanne still had moments of panic. Not about Stephen and their love. Never about that. But about everything she wanted to live up to in him.

''Is my veil straight? Is my makeup smudged? Is my train crumpled? I'm going to take another look in the mirror....''

Cat and Jill spent several more minutes fussing over her.

''And now you must come,'' Natalya said softly. ''Because Stephen is waiting....''

He was waiting with ill-concealed impatience, as it happened, at the altar of Saint Catherine's Cathedral.

''Where is she?'' he hissed to Arkady Radouleau, who was acting as his best man.

''Brides are always late.''

''She wasn't late the first time we did this. She was early!''

"She wasn't in love with you, then," Arkady pointed out patiently.

"Does that make a difference?"

"All the difference in the world."

"But in the other direction, I'd have thought," Stephen complained, his agitation mounting, "that she, perhaps, couldn't bear to be away from me for a second longer than necessary, which is the way I feel about her, now and every moment of every day!"

"Your Highness," Arkady soothed him, "she wants to look perfect for you."

"She could do that in a pair of flannel pajamas, with a heavy dose of flu!"

At this, Arkady Radouleau just laughed, the hearty sound echoing in this great space, above the sibilant whispers of the crowded congregation.

Then they both heard the wheezy swell of organ music, and the bridal march began. Stephen's breath caught painfully in his lungs. Here was Suzanne, no longer the shy, single-minded bride with the white, determined face, a woman he hardly knew, who had come toward him on her stepfather's arm, more than three months ago, but the woman he loved to the depth of his soul.

She was beautiful, warm, courageous, thoughtful. She had already astonished him with her rapid progress in the Aragovian language. She had made over Princess Alice's entire fortune to an inviolable trust for building Aragovia's education system and its public library facilities. She was a woman who could love Alice and love him and forgive Rose—who had arrived from America several days ago, and stood now with Perry in the front row of the congregation—and make him happier than he had ever thought he could be.

The music died away. The archbishop of Aragovia began the lengthy formal ceremony. There were hymns, a sermon, prayers and vows. Suzanne lifted her veil and at last…*at last*…Stephen kissed her, half drowning in the light of happiness glowing in her eyes.

Standing just to one side, the two silk-clad matrons of honor leaned closer to each other as the kiss went on…and on…then softly broke apart.

"Are you still scared about this?" Jill said to Cat. "Do you still want to ask her about how she feels?"

"No, I'm not scared," Cat said.

"No…"

"She's happy. We don't need to ask. I can feel the radiance from here."

A few minutes later, Their Royal Highnesses Prince Stephen and Princess Suzanne of Aragovia set off from the cathedral steps in their open coach, pulled through the streets of the capital by four silver-gray horses, showing a smiling Princess Alice to the cheering crowds.

"Will you let me keep you happy ever after?" Stephen whispered to his bride.

"Yes," she answered simply, and that one little word was all that counted, so she said it again, with tears in her eyes. "Yes, Stephen, I will."

* * * * *

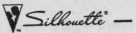